M

THE HEAVENS OPENED

He looked down at her face for a long moment, as if he wished to engrave it on his memory forever, then as his arms tightened his lips sought hers.

It was as if the Heavens opened, and she knew an inexpressible ecstasy that was beyond all thought or imagination.

He kissed her gently at first, as if she was something infinitely precious, then the softness of her mouth aroused him in a way he had never known before.

Bantam Books by Barbara Cartland
Ask your bookseller for the books you have missed

Barbara Cartland's Library of Love Series

A Night Of Gaiety

Barbara Cartland

A NIGHT OF GAIETY

A Bantam Book / July 1981

ISBN O-553-14791-9

Published simultaneously in the United States and Canada

Bantam Books are published by Bantam Books, Inc. Its trade-
mark, consisting of the words ''Bantam Books'' and the por-
trayal of bantam is Registered in U.S. Patent and Trademark
Office and in other countries. Marca Registrada. Bantam
Books, Inc., 666 Fifth Avenue, New York, New York 10103.

PRINTED   IN   THE   UNITED   STATES   OF   AMERICA

0 9 8 7 6 5 4 3 2 1

Author's Note

I knew many of the Gaiety Girls when I came out in the 1920s. One dear friend was the Marchioness of Headfort, who was Rosie Boote. She came from Tipperary and her father had been a gentleman of independent means. She first appeared in *The Shop Girl* in 1895. She worked hard, never slacked, and never gave an indifferent performance.

The Marquis of Headfort had a prominent place in the Irish Peerage and was very popular at Court. His family strenuously opposed the marriage; but Rosie stepped into her high position with such grace and charm that everyone loved her. She and her husband were very happy.

I knew the Countess Poulett, who was Sylvia Storey, and the lovely Denise Orme, who married first Lord Churston and as her third husband the Duke of Leinster, but my greatest friend was the fascinating Zena Dare.

She married the Hon. Maurice Brett, and one of their daughters was one of my bridesmaids. After her husband's death, Zena went back on the stage and played in *My Fair Lady* for nine years, as the mother of Professor Higgins, without missing a performance.

She only gave up when she was over eighty but still slim, lovely, fascinating, and carried herself magnificently, like a goddess—or should I say, a Gaiety Girl?

Chapter One
1891

"Is that all?" Davita asked.

"I am afraid so, Miss Kilcraig," the Solicitor replied. "It is extremely regrettable that your father was so extravagant during the last years of his life. I am afraid he ignored any suggestions from me or my partners that he should economise."

Davita did not reply because she knew that what Mr. Stirling was saying was that this last year her father had been so intent on drinking away his sorrows that he did not heed anything anybody said to him.

More than once she had tried to talk to him about their financial position, but he would always tell her not to interfere, and now that he was dead, what she had feared had happened.

The bills had mounted and mounted.

They had been bad enough before her Stepmother had left, but afterwards her father had seemed to enjoy throwing his money about in ridiculous ways, or else being too sodden with whisky to know what he was doing.

But even in her most depressed moment, Davita had not imagined that she would find herself with just under two hundred pounds and literally nothing else.

The Castle which had belonged to the Kilcraigs for several hundred years had been mortgaged up to the hilt, and what was left of the furniture had now been sold.

The better pieces, like the paintings and some rather fine gold-framed mirrors, her father had already sold soon after he married Katie Kingston.

This past year when her father had become more and more irresponsible, Davita had often thought that she should hate her Stepmother, but instead she could not help feeling that in many ways there was a good excuse for her behaviour.

After her own mother had died three years ago, when Davita was only fifteen, her father had found the loneliness intolerable, and he had gone off first to Edinburgh and then to London in search of amusement.

Davita had thought even then that she could understand that her father had often craved for the gay life he had known as a young man in London before he had inherited the Baronetcy and come to Scotland to marry and what people called "settle down."

Because he had been very much in love with his wife, he had found it tolerable to live in an ancient, crumbling Castle with a thousand unproductive acres of moorland and only a few neighbours.

Somehow he and Davita's mother had managed to amuse themselves, fishing in the river, shooting over the moors, and every so often going off on a spree to Edinburgh and even occasionally to London.

But her mother worried because these trips cost money.

"We cannot really afford it, Iain," she would say when her husband suggested they should leave Davita in charge of the servants and have what he called a "second honeymoon."

"We are only young once," he would reply.

Then her mother would forget her qualms of conscience,

there would be a scuffle to get their best clothes packed, and they would drive away looking, Davita thought, very much like a honeymoon couple.

Then her mother had died one cold winter when the winds blowing from the North Sea and down from the snow-peaked mountains seemed to catch at one's throat.

Her father had been so distraught that it had in fact been a relief when he said he could stand the gloom of Scotland no longer and intended to go South.

"Go to London, Papa, and see your friends," Davita had said. "I shall be all right, and when I am older perhaps I shall be able to come with you."

Her father had smiled.

"I do not think you would be able to accompany me to any of my old haunts," he had said, "but I will think about it. In the meantime, get on with your lessons. You might just as well be clever as well as beautiful."

Davita had flushed at the word because she thought it a compliment, but she knew that she did in fact resemble her mother, and no-one could ever deny that Lady Kilcraig had been a very beautiful woman.

When Davita looked up at the portrait of her mother which hung over the mantelpiece in the Drawing-Room, she would pray that she would grow more and more like her.

They had the same colour hair with its fiery lights, and it was certainly not the ugly, gingery red that was characteristic of so many Scots. It was the deep red of the first autumn leaves which seemed to hold the sunshine.

Her eyes, again like her mother's, were grey in some lights and green in others, and, where Davita was concerned, they were clear and innocent as a trout-stream.

Because she was very young she had a child-like beauty. It may have been the curves of her face or the softness of her mouth, but there was something flower-like about her which belied her red hair and the green of her eyes.

"With your colouring," her father once said, "you ought

to look like a seductive siren. But instead, my sweet, you look like a fairy-child who has been left behind amidst the toad-stools where the fairies dance."

Davita had always loved it when her father talked to her of the myths and stories that circulated amongst the Scottish crofters.

They had learnt them from the Bards, and in the long winter evenings they told their children tales of the feuds between the Chieftains, interspersed with legends, superstitions, and stories which were all a part of their being "fey."

It had been so much a part of her own childhood that she often found it difficult to know where her knowledge ended and her imagination began.

Her mother added to her fantasies because her parents, both Scots, came from the Western Isles and her grandmother had been Irish.

"Your mother brought the leprechauns with her!" her father would sometimes say teasingly, when something vanished mysteriously or her mother had a presentiment that something strange was going to happen.

Davita had not been able to comfort her father in his grief, and now she imagined that she had been partially to blame for the fact that, desperate in his loneliness, he had married again when he was in London.

It had seemed inconceivable that he should have chosen as his second wife a Gaiety Girl, but when Davita saw Katie Kingston, which had been her stage-name, after the first shock of finding that any woman had taken her mother's place, and an actress at that, she had liked her.

She was certainly very attractive, although her mascaraed eye-lashes, her crimson mouth, and her rouged cheeks had been somewhat of a surprise in Scotland.

But her laughter and her voice, which had a distinct lilt in it, seemed to vibrate through the house like sunshine coming through the clouds.

Then, as might have been expected, Katie began to be bored.

Davita could understand that it had been one thing in London to marry a Baronet with all the leading actors and actresses of the Gaiety present, but quite another to have no audience but a few crofters, a stepdaughter, and a husband who, now that he was home, occupied most of his hours with sport.

"What shall we do today?" she would ask Davita as she sat up in the big oak four-poster bed, eating her breakfast and looking somewhat disconsolately out the window at the moors.

"What do you want to do?" Davita would ask.

"If I were in London," her Stepmother replied, "I'd go shopping in Bond Street, promenade down Regent's Street, and then have lunch with an admirer at Romano's."

She gave a little sigh before she went on:

"Best of all, I would know that at six o'clock this evening I should be popping in at the stage-door and climbing up to my dressing-room to put on my make-up."

There was a yearning note in her voice which Davita began to listen for, and it would intensify as she went on to relate what it was like behind the scenes of the Gaiety.

Katie was already thirty-six—which was another reason why she had married while she had the chance—so she had seen many of the great changes that had taken place at the Gaiety over the years.

"You've never seen anything like it," she told Davita once, "when Hollingshead, who was the Boss in those days, installed electric light at the Theatre."

Katie's blue eyes were gleaming as she went on:

"It was nine o'clock on August second in 1878 that the current was switched on. Lamps sizzled and flickered, then it brought the crowds hurrying into the Strand to look at the Gaiety."

It was not only the Theatre she described to Davita; she would tell her about the Stage-Door Johnnies, young

men who would arrive in hansoms, "all dolled up" with
their evening-dress capes, their silk Opera-hats, white
gloves in their hands, and patent-leather boots shining
like jet.

"They were all waiting after the Show to take us out to
supper," Katie would say rapturously. "They sent flowers that filled the dressing-rooms and often gave us expensive presents."

"It must have been very exciting!" Davita would cry
breathlessly.

"There's never been actresses anywhere in the world
that had the glamour and the allure of us Gaiety Girls!"
Katie boasted. "The newspapers say that we're the 'Spir-
it of the London Gaiety incarnate,' and that's what we
are! The Guv'nor knows that we bring in the Nobs to the
Theatre, so he doesn't economise on us, oh no! Only the
best for a Gaiety Girl!"

Katie would show Davita her gowns that she wore on
stage, some of which had been a present from the
"Guv'nor," George Edwardes, when she left.

They were all made of the most expensive silks and
satins, her petticoats were trimmed with real lace, and
her hats were ornamented with the finest ostrich-feathers
obtainable.

"We Gaiety Girls are famous!" Katie boasted.

Davita began to understand that what Katie was saying
was that whether a man was rich or poor, young or elderly, to take a Gaiety Girl out to supper, to drive her home
in a hansom, or to propel her in a punt at Maidenhead
was to touch the wings of ecstatic romance.

What Katie did not tell Davita, Hector, who had been
her father's valet for years and was now getting old,
added after she was gone.

"Ye canna cage a song-bird, Miss Davita," he had said
with his broad Scots accent. "Them Gaiety gals are not
like th' other actresses. Th' gentlemen go mad over 'em
and it's no surprising."

"Are they really so lovely, Hector?" Davita asked curiously.

"They be chosen for their looks," Hector said, "but some o' them are canny as weel, and there's nothing of the old Music Hall aboot them."

It took Davita some time to understand that the women who performed at the Music Hall were often coarse and vulgar, while the Gaiety Girls were ostensibly lady-like and refined.

Not that she found Katie particularly refined when she compared her with her mother.

At the same time, she could understand that it was her *joie de vivre* which her father had found fascinating and which had made him determined that he would not return to Scotland without her.

While Katie was struggling to adjust herself to her new life—Davita knew she had at first made a real effort—it was Violet, her daughter, who faced facts fairly and squarely when, six months after the marriage, she arrived to stay.

If Davita had thought her Stepmother attractive, she found herself staring wide-eyed at Violet.

She learnt that there were always eight outstandingly beautiful girls in every Gaiety production who moved about the stage wearing gorgeous gowns but were not performers in any other way.

They were not part of the *corps de ballet*, nor did they have anything to say; they just looked and were beautiful.

Violet was one of these, and when she appeared in Scotland she seemed to Davita like a goddess from another planet.

She had fair hair and blue eyes like her mother, her features were perfect, and when she smiled it was as if the *Venus de Milo* had suddenly become human.

"Why, I could hardly believe my eyes when I got your telegram!" Katie exclaimed, flinging her arms round her daughter.

"We've got a fortnight's holiday before we start re-hearsals for the next Show, and I thought I'd come and see you. I've brought Harry with me. I hope you can put us up?"

Harry was an exceedingly handsome actor, and Katie made him as welcome as her daughter.

"He's getting on a bit," she said to Davita when they were talking about him. "He wants to 'go straight' rather than keep to the Juvenile leads which entail so much singing and dancing."

Harry had done well and had been billed as leading-man in the last three Shows at the Gaiety, besides becoming a draw at the Music Halls.

He seemed to have more to say to Katie than to her daughter, and it had been left to Davita to entertain Violet.

"Do you like the Theatre?" she had asked.

Violet's blue eyes lit up.

"I adore it! I'd not leave the Gaiety if a Duke asked me to run away with him, let alone a Baronet!"

She spoke without thinking, and added apologetically:

"I suppose I shouldn't have said that."

"I understand," Davita said with a smile.

"I don't know how Mum sticks it," Violet went on. "All this space!"

She looked out over the moors.

"I like to see houses out the window. You must be cut off here in the winter."

Davita laughed.

"You will be back in London before that."

"I sincerely hope so!" Violet exclaimed fervently.

"Your mother is very happy with my father," Davita said quickly, "although she misses London sometimes."

"I'm not surprised!"

Violet made herself very pleasant and Davita liked her.

Actually there was not very much difference in their ages, because Violet, having been, as Katie said "a little mistake" when she was only seventeen, had just passed her eighteenth birthday.

Davita could never quite understand what had happened to her father, Katie's first husband, whose name had been Lock.

"Good-looking he was," Katie had once said reminiscently, "with dark eyes that always seemed to have a smouldering fire in them, and that's why the audience went mad about him! But Lord knows he was dull when he got home! I was very young and very stupid, but Violet's got her head screwed on all right. I've seen to that!"

Davita did not quite understand the innuendoes in this conversation, but she gathered that Mr. Lock had left Katie before Violet was born.

Although she had never seen him again, he had not died until three years ago, leaving Katie free to marry Sir Iain Kilcraig.

"It must have been very difficult for you bringing up Violet all by yourself," Davita said sympathetically.

"I was lucky, I had very good—friends," Katie said briefly, and left it at that.

Violet learnt to fish while she was staying in Scotland. She soon picked up the art of casting and was thrilled with the first salmon she caught.

Davita persuaded her to walk up to the top of the moors and for a short time she forgot that she was an actress from the Gaiety Theatre and became just a young girl enjoying the exercise and, when it grew hot, paddling with Davita in the burns.

They went riding on the sure-footed small ponies that Davita had ridden ever since she was a child, talked to the crofters, and shopped in the village which was over two miles from the Castle.

It was only afterwards that Davita realised that while she was enjoying her time with Violet, Katie was spending her time with Harry.

Her father had been busy because it was the lambing season and he always made a point of assisting the shepherds. Moreover, unfortunately as it turned out, there was a run of salmon, which meant that the fishing was good, and he had spent a good part of each day by the river.

Even so, Davita thought that what happened was inevitable and it was only a question of Katie finding the right moment.

Soon after Violet had returned to London and Harry went with her, Katie disappeared.

She left a note for her husband saying that she had an irresistible urge to see her friends, and she had not told him so to his face because she could not face a scene! She promised to write to him later.

When she did write, and the letter arrived just as Sir Iain was determined to go and find her, it was to say that she was sorry but she could not leave the stage.

She had the chance of going to America with a part on Broadway, and it was something she could not refuse.

It was Hector who revealed that that was where Harry also had gone.

"He talked aboot it a great deal, Miss Davita, while I was putting out his clothes. He said it was the chance of a lifetime an' something he'd no intention o' missing."

In a way, Davita could understand that it had been the "chance of a lifetime" for Katie as well, but her father behaved at first like a madman, then settled down to drown his sorrows.

He died of pneumonia, caught because he had fallen into a ditch on his way back from the village where he had gone to buy more whisky.

He had apparently been so drunk that he lay there all night, and in the morning a shepherd found him and helped him home. But the cold he caught turned to pneumonia, and when Davita called the Doctor there was nothing he could do.

Davita now realised with a shock that she had been left penniless, although it was satisfactory that Hector had been provided for.

Her father had left him a small croft with a pension, separated from everything else which had been pooled to meet his debts.

When Davita looked at the bills she had been appalled at what her father had managed to spend in London during the time he had spent there after her mother's death.

There were bills for champagne, for flowers, for gowns, hats, furs, sun-shades, all of which she presumed he had given to Katie.

There was also an account from a Jeweller's, and bills for his own clothes which seemed astronomical.

Again in her imagination she could understand that her father would have wanted to be smart, dashing, and young, as he had been in the days before he first married.

Then he had his own hansom-cab always waiting for him, belonged to the best Clubs, and dined every night, naturally not alone, at Romano's, Rules, or The Continental.

But now Davita was alone, and it was frightening to think that everything that was familiar, everything that had been her background ever since she was a child, was no longer hers.

Mr. Stirling put into words the question that was in her mind.

"What are you going to do, Miss Kilcraig?"

Davita made a helpless little gesture with her hands, and the elderly man watching her thought how young she was and how very lovely.

It struck him that she was like a beautiful, exotic flower, and he had the uncomfortable feeling that she might not transplant.

"Surely you must have some relations?" he asked gently.

"Papa's sister, who was older than he was, is dead," Davita answered. "I had a Great-Aunt who lived in Edinburgh, but she died a long time ago, and I never remember meeting any of Mama's family because they lived so far away."

"You could write to them," Mr. Stirling suggested.

"It would be very embarrassing if I tried to foist myself on them," Davita answered, "and I do not think they are well off."

When she thought about it, the Western Isles seemed to be in another world.

"You cannot stay here," Mr. Stirling said, "so I am afraid you will have to find either a relative with whom you can live, or some sort of employment."

"Employment?" Davita queried. "But I am not certain what I could do."

"One of my partners might be able to suggest something," Mr. Stirling suggested. "There must be employment in Edinburgh for a young lady like yourself, but for the moment I cannot think what it could be."

"It is very kind of you to think of it," Davita said with a smile, "but although Papa always insisted I should be well educated, it seems extraordinary that nothing I have learnt seems likely to be saleable."

Davita gave him a brief little smile as if she was determined to make light of her difficulties.

"Of course the best thing would be for you to be married," Mr. Stirling said.

"That would be rather difficult," Davita replied, "as nobody has asked me."

That, she thought, was not surprising, since there were no young men in the vicinity, and she had never stayed in Edinburgh for any length of time, nor, after her mother's death, had she made contact with the few friends they had there.

"I tell you what I will do," Mr. Stirling said. "I will have a talk with my wife and the wives of my partners. Perhaps you could look after children or something of that sort."

"It is very kind of you," Davita replied, "very, very kind, and I am most grateful."

"You will be hearing from me."

The carriage was waiting to drive him to the Station, and as he drove away, raising his old-fashioned, low top-hat, Davita thought he looked like one of the Elders of the Church, and her heart sank.

She could imagine all too clearly what his wife and the wives of his partners would look like, and she was quite sure they would disapprove of her because she looked so young, just as they disapproved because her father had married a Gaiety Girl.

She knew that the stage was considered extremely disreputable, especially in Scotland, and she could al-most see the ladies in Edinburgh wringing their hands in horror because she had been associated with anyone so reprehensible as an actress from the Gaiety Theatre.

'What am I to do? What *am* I to do?' she questioned.

Because she was frightened for her future, she went in search of Hector.

He was packing up her father's clothes, and as she entered the bedroom he looked up from the leather trunk beside which he was kneeling to ask:

"Has the gentleman gone, Miss Davita?"

"Yes," Davita answered, "and as we both expected, Hector, he brought bad news."

"I was afraid o' that, Miss Davita," Hector said, "an' it's awful hard on ye."

Davita had no secrets from Hector, he knew her fi-nancial position, and he had in fact explained a great deal to her before Mr. Stirling had arrived.

"When everything is cleared up," Davita said, sitting down on the edge of the bed, "I shall have precisely one hundred ninety-six pounds, ten shillings!"

"Well, that's better than nought," Hector remarked.

"Yes, I know," Davita replied, "but it will not last forever, and I shall have to find work of some sort, Hector. But what can I do?"

"Work, Miss Davita?"

Hector sat back on his heels and it was obvious that this had not occurred to him before.

"Either that, or live on air, which I do not believe is very substantial fare," Davita said.

"Now suppose for th' time being ye have me croft, Miss Davita?" Hector said. "I've still got a few years o' work left in me, an'...."

Davita gave a little cry and interrupted him before he could say any more.

"Do not be so ridiculous, Hector!" she said. "It is sweet of you, and just like your kind heart, but you know as well as I do that you should not go on working any longer, and Papa was sensible enough to give you a croft and leave you enough money so that you will not starve."

She paused to say in a more practical tone:

"All the same, there will be work at the Castle to employ you for a few days a week, which will provide you with the luxuries you could not otherwise afford."

"I don't need much, Miss Davita," Hector replied, "and there's always a wee rabbit or a grouse up th' hill."

Davita laughed, and they both knew he intended to poach what he required.

"If it comes to that," he said, "there'll be enough for two. I'm not a big eater."

"You are the kindest man in the world," Davita replied, "but we have to be sensible, Hector. I cannot stay with you for the rest of my life, and at eighteen I have to learn to look after myself."

She gave a little sigh.

"Not that it would be very exciting being in Edinburgh with Mrs. Stirling!"

"Is that what he suggested?" Hector enquired.

"Something of the . . . sort."

She knew by the expression on the old man's face that he was thinking, as she had, that Mrs. Stirling would disapprove of her father having died as he had, and more especially of Katie.

Davita felt she could almost hear the whispers:

"You can't touch pitch without being defiled!"

"Those who sup with the Devil should use a long spoon!"

She wanted to cry out that she could not bear it, and she felt she would be quite incapable of controlling young children and making them obey her.

"Oh, Hector, what shall I . . . do?" she asked.

Then as she looked down at what he was packing she saw in the trunk a picture of Katie.

It was in a silver frame and Hector had laid it on top of one of her father's suits and obviously intended to cover it with another so that there was no possibility of the glass breaking.

Davita had heard from Katie all about the photographic beauties whose faces filled the illustrated papers and show-windows.

Katie had been photographed for advertisements and, like Maude Branscombe, who had been the first of the beauties, had posed for a religious picture.

"Very pretty I looked," she had told Davita, "wearing a kind of nightgown with my hair hanging over my shoulders, and clinging to a cross!"

Then she had laughed the light, spontaneous laugh which had always delighted Sir Iain.

"I wonder what some of those old battle-axes who took my picture into their pious homes would feel if they knew it was a Gaiety Girl they were pressing in their Bibles or hanging on the wall!"

Katie had laughed again.

"That picture brought me in a lot of shiny golden sovereigns, and that's what mattered!"

It was then, looking at Katie's photograph, that Davita had an idea.

What was the point of being looked down on and perhaps despised in Edinburgh?

If she had to work, she was much more likely to find it in London than anywhere else.

She would go to Violet, who had been very friendly all the time she was staying with her, and in fact at times she had seemed almost like the sister Davita had never had.

She remembered too that Violet had said to her:

"You're very pretty, Davita, and in a year or two you'll be stunning! If you take my advice, you'll not waste yourself in this dead-or-alive place."

"But this is my home!" Davita had said.

"Home or not, the moors aren't going to pay you compliments, and the only kisses you'll get will be from the wind, which anyway will ruin your skin!"

Davita had laughed, but when Violet had gone she had missed her.

It had been fun to have another girl of almost the same age to talk to, while she knew that her father, when he was with Katie, found her rather an encumbrance.

Afterwards, when he was sober enough he clung to her because there was no-one else.

"If you think I want that woman back, you are mistaken!" he would say angrily. "I'll show her I can do without her! This is my home, and if it is not good enough for her, she can go and jump in the sea for all I care!"

His violent mood would then give way to self-pity and a little while later he would cry:

"I miss her, Davita! You are a good child and I am fond of you, but a man wants a woman in his life, and she was so pretty! I liked to hear her laugh. I wish you had seen her on the stage; I could not look at anybody else when she was there."

He would go on and on for hours, until once, without thinking, Davita had said:

"Why do you not go to London, Papa? It would cheer you up."

Her father had turned on her angrily.

"Do you suppose I have not thought of that? Do you suppose I wish to be stuck in this benighted place? Dammit all, London would help me to forget—of course it would—but I have not the money. Do you understand, Davita? I have not a penny to my name!"

Davita could almost hear him now, shouting the words at her, and they seemed to be still echoing round the room.

Then as Hector put a neatly folded suit over Katie Kingston's photograph, she made up her mind.

"I am going to London, Hector!" she said quietly. "If Miss Violet cannot help me to find work, then I will come back."

* * *

The train in which Davita was travelling from Edinburgh was uncomfortably crowded for the first part of the journey.

Then gradually, as passengers got out at every stop, Davita found herself alone, with the exception of one other woman, in the carriage marked: *"Ladies Only."*

It was Hector who had insisted she should travel Second-Class.

"I think it is too extravagant," Davita had said, thinking how long her money had to last.

"I'm not having ye, Miss Davita, going off on yer own in a Third-Class carriage with th' type of scum that's sometimes in 'em!" Hector replied.

Although Davita knew he was talking good sense, she parted reluctantly with what seemed to her a lot of money, and left Hector to find her a corner seat and make sure her trunk was placed in the Guard's-Van.

As she waved him good-bye she felt as if she was leaving behind her in Scotland not only everything she loved but also her childhood.

Now she was on her own, grown up, a woman who should take care of herself, but somehow she had not the least idea how to set about it.

Then she thought that if things got too frightening, she could go back to Hector and stay with him in his tiny croft until she could start again.

It consisted of only two rooms, one up and one down, but she knew it would not worry Hector to sleep in the lower room while she occupied the only bedroom.

He would look after her as he had looked after her father from the time he was a boy, and her mother when they were married.

But Hector was growing old, and she had to be sensible and start to find her own way in the world, as many other young women had done before her.

But deep down inside she was frightened, and she found herself wishing, as she had so often before in her life, that she had been the boy her mother had expected, who was to have been called "David," which was a family name, instead of being a girl and an only child at that.

She had brought with her the only possessions she owned, and they filled exactly two trunks.

After her mother's death she had fortunately kept her clothes and altered them to fit herself.

But she was quite sure, even though they were made of good materials and some of them came from the best shops in Edinburgh, that by now they would be out of fashion.

Katie's clothes had of course been very different.

At the same time, while she had been living with them Davita had taken the opportunity of altering some of her mother's gowns to make them more fashionable.

Katie had also occasionally thrown a gown at Davita and said:

"Here, you take this! I'll never wear it again, and although it's too big for you, the stuff's good—the Guv'nor saw to that!"

Davita had managed to make herself two gowns out of Katie's cast-offs, but the third was of crimson taffeta, which was a hopeless contrast to her hair.

She did not dare spend one penny of her precious inheritance on clothes, so she merely wore a travelling-gown and cape which had belonged to her mother, and changed the ribbons and feathers from one bonnet to another to make what she hoped was a suitable ensemble in which to appear in London.

As the train drew nearer and nearer to the Metropolis, Davita became more and more frightened.

She had never been to London before, but from all she had heard about it, she suddenly felt that she had made a mistake and would much better have stayed in the world to which she belonged, however lonely it might have been.

Her father had extolled London as if it were a Paradise of gaiety and excitement, with dashing, handsome men and beautiful, alluring women.

But he was a man, and from some of the things Katie had told her, Davita had been well aware that for a woman without money life could be a struggle with a lot of danger about it that she did not completely understand.

"I had a hard time on me own with Violet to look after, and no job until I got back my health and strength, and my figure too, when it came to that."

"Surely your husband . . . ?" Davita began.

"He'd gone—scuttled!" Katie said. "He was the sort who never ought to have got married. I was a fool to listen to him, but when you're in love . . ."

She had spoken derisively, then with one of her lilting little laughs she had added:

"I never learn, do I? Here I am at thirty-six, letting me heart rule me head once again, and where's it got me? To bonnie Scotland, and not so bonnie from what I've seen of it!"

Davita had laughed, but she had thought then that there was a little note of desperation in Katie's voice, which had worried her.

Katie had left for America with not only her experience of the stage to help her but also Harry.

Afterwards, Davita thought she might have expected that Katie was infatuated with the handsome actor, from the way she looked at him all the time he had been staying with them.

She had thought innocently that it was because he was a great actor and, as Violet had described him, a "star."

But after Katie was gone she supposed that the expression in her blue eyes had been one of love, and she thought the way Harry had looked at her had explained why the women at the matinees had watched him breathlessly and found their hearts beating quicker.

Katie would be all right, Davita thought, and wondered how she could let her know she was now a widow.

Then she remembered that she was going to see Violet, who would undoubtedly know where her mother was to be found.

Again Davita felt a little quiver of fear.

Suppose Violet did not want her? Suppose she was angry with her for coming South without waiting for a reply to her letters?

Davita had written to her ten days ago, but she had not actually expected Violet to answer, because she remembered her saying several times when she had been staying with them:

"I can't bear writing letters or anything else for that

matter! I learnt enough at School to read, but writing's hard work, and besides, I can't spell!"

"Better not let the Guv'nor hear you talking like that!" Katie had exclaimed. "You know he likes his girls to be ladylike, and ladies always say 'thank you' properly."

"I don't know what you mean by 'properly,' " Violet had replied. "I'd rather say 'thank you' with a kiss than write."

Katie had laughed.

"That's a different thing! But if a Duke asks you out to supper, you can hardly send him a kiss to say 'yes.' "

"I manage!" Violet answered, and they both had laughed.

Davita thought now that if Violet refused to have her, she would have to try to find a Domestic Bureau.

She remembered her mother talking about them once and saying that servants in the South and in Edinburgh could be obtained from Bureaus which brought employers and employees together.

"What a strange idea!" Davita had exclaimed. She had been very young at the time.

"Not really," her mother had answered. "If you want a Cook, for instance, you can hardly put a notice-board outside your house saying 'Cook Wanted.' "

"If you did, you might get hundreds and hundreds of applicants for the position!" Davita had laughed.

"And that would certainly be a nuisance," Lady Kil-craig had replied with a smile. "So, grand ladies go to a Bureau when they want a Cook, a house-maid, a Gover-ness, or a footman, and the servants sit on hard benches hoping someone will require their services and pay them well and be kind masters."

Davita remembered at the time thinking it was a strange way of doing things, but now she told herself that that was what she would have to do—sit on a hard bench until somebody came in who said:

"I want a young, inexperienced girl with no particular talents, but I will pay her and be kind to her if she will come into my employment."

"That would certainly have to be a very eccentric and very exceptional sort of person," she told herself.

She felt panic rising within her as they passed through the suburbs and she realised they would soon be steaming into St. Pancras Station.

It was Hector, who had travelled a great deal in his life, who had made the journey far more comfortable than it would have been otherwise.

He had packed her a small picnic-basket with enough food to ensure that she would not be hungry before she reached London.

He had even provided her with a bottle of cold tea, saying it was nicer than water, and if she tried to buy food in the Stations she might get involved with rowdy or unpleasant men.

He had also made her take a rug to cover her knees in case she was cold at night. It had been difficult to sleep because of the noise and the movement of the train, had she knew how sensible he had been.

Now she put on her bonnet, tidied her hair, and wished she could wash before she went in search of Violet.

She knew, as it was getting late in the afternoon, that the sooner she reached her destination the better.

Fortunately, Violet had given her her address when she had said good-bye at the Castle.

"If I've left anything behind, be a sport and post it to me," she said. "I lost one of my brooches at the last place I stayed and they never sent it on to me."

"Do you mean they kept it?" Davita asked in amazement.

"I wouldn't be surprised."

"Well, I promise anything I find I will post to you at once!"

Davita had written down Violet's address, and although she had found nothing to send on, she had kept a note of it.

Now she remembered that it was some time ago and perhaps Violet would have gone elsewhere.

It was the first time this idea had suggested itself, and Davita was more frightened than she had been before.

As the train steamed into the Station and drew up at the platform, she felt it was impossible for her to leave the carriage.

Then a porter was shouting at the window and she forced herself to ask him to find her trunks for her. He picked up her picnic-basket and the small bag in which she had carried the few things which would not fit into her trunk, then set off in the direction of the Guard's-Van.

Carrying her rug over one arm, with her handbag in the other, Davita followed him down the platform, feeling that there were far too many people and the noise was deafening.

Then, the porter having kindly looked after her, Davita found herself driving away from the Station in a four-wheeler, her trunks perched on the top of it, with a rather tired horse carrying her through the crowded streets.

"I am here!" she said to herself. "I am in London, and please . . . please, God . . . take care of me!"

Chapter Two

The house looked rather dingy and gloomy on the outside and Davita told herself it was because she was not used to London houses.

She asked the cabman who had climbed down from his box to wait, and went up two steps to raise the knocker which she noted needed polishing.

There was some delay before the door was opened, and a rather blowsy but pleasant-looking woman stood facing her.

"Could I please . . . speak to . . . Miss Violet Lock?" Davita asked in a voice that sounded somewhat hesitating.

The woman smiled.

"I thinks yer must be the friend her's expectin' from Scotland," she said with a Cockney accent.

For a moment Davita felt such a wave of relief sweep over her that it was difficult to speak. Then she said:

"Yes . . . I am . . . Is Miss Lock . . . here?"

"You've just missed her, dearie, she's gorn to the Theatre," the woman replied. "I'm Mrs. Jenkins, an' I gathers I'm to expec' a new lodger."

"I should be very grateful if I could stay here," Davita replied.

The Landlady had already pushed past her to shout to the cabby outside:

"Bring 'em up t' the Second Floor back, there's a good man!"

Davita thought the cabman grumbled at the instructions, but she did not wait to hear as she followed Mrs. Jenkins up the stairs.

They were narrow and the carpet was worn, but she could think of nothing but the joy of knowing that Violet had expected her and she was not, as she had been half-afraid, alone in London with nowhere to go.

When they reached the second floor, Mrs. Jenkins opened a door at the back and Davita almost gasped as she saw the tiniest room she had ever been expected to sleep in.

There was just room for one bedstead and a rather rickety-looking chest-of-drawers. There was a rag-mat on the soiled linoleum.

"It's a bit small," Mrs. Jenkins said, which was an understatement, "but yer friend's next door, and I feels yer'd rather be near 'er than up another flight."

"Yes ... of course," Davita said quckly, "and it was very kind of you to think of it."

Mrs. Jenkins smiled at her.

"I tries to 'elp," she answered, "an' I never tikes a lodger in what ain't on the boards. Yer're the exception, but wiv yer looks yer'll soon find yersel' a place at the Gaiety."

She looked at Davita appraisingly as she spoke, taking in the red hair under her bonnet, the clear petal-like skin, and her large, rather frightened eyes.

"Yer're pretty enough—I'll say that for yer," she said. "Can yer dance?"

"I ... I am afraid not," Davita answered. "And I would be far too nervous to go on the stage, besides ..."

She was just about to say that it was something of which her mother would not have approved, then she thought it would be a mistake to do so.

Mrs. Jenkins laughed.

"If yer gets the chance, yer'll jump at it!"

Davita did not have to reply, because at that moment
the cabman, breathing heavily, came up the stairs with
one of her trunks on his back.

It was impossible for him to get it into the room unless
they both moved into the passage, and when finally he
brought up the other trunk, Davita thought she would
have to climb over them to get into bed.

Then, having paid the cabman, as she stood looking
rather helplessly at her trunks, Mrs. Jenkins said:

"Now what yer'd better do, dearie, is change yer
clothes, clean yerself up a bit, nip round to the Theatre,
an' tell Violet yer're 'ere."

"G-go to the . . . Theatre?" Davita questioned.

"Yeah. Billy'll get yer a hackney-carriage when yer're
ready, an' yer tell 'im to go to the stage-door. Yer'll find
'er in 'er dressing-room. The Show don't start for another
'our."

Because Mrs. Jenkins spoke so positively, Davita did
not dare to argue with her.

Instead, as the Landlady went down the stairs, she
obediently took off her travelling-gown and cape, and
found in one of her trunks a pretty afternoon-gown which
was not too creased.

It had belonged to her mother, and she had altered it
to look a little more fashionable, copying one of the gowns
which Katie had brought North with her.

When she was ready, Davita looked very pretty. Katie
had told her that everybody in London always wore a hat
in the evening unless they were going to a Ball, so she
took one from her hat-box.

It was a hat which Katie had given her and which she
had thought she would never wear because it was far too
smart and over-decorated for Scotland.

Even now she hesitated after she had put it on, thinking as she looked at herself in the mirror that if she

appeared in the Kirk in such a creation, the Congregation would either be scandalised or would laugh at her.

Quickly she removed two of the ostrich-feathers, and when she thought she looked comparatively ordinary and her appearance was unlikely to cause comment, she picked up her handbag and went rather nervously down the stairs.

She had difficulty finding Mrs. Jenkins. Then, hearing a noise from the basement, she descended to find her in a large, dark kitchen, cooking on an old-fashioned range.

"Excuse me . . ." Davita began nervously.

Mrs. Jenkins turned round.

"Oh, there yer are, dearie," she exclaimed, "quicker'n I expected!"

"Do I . . . do I look . . . all right?" Davita asked hesitatingly.

"O' course yer do!" Mrs. Jenkins replied. "A bit plain for th' Gaiety, but London'll soon smarten yer up, don't yer worry about that!"

She suddenly shouted so loudly at the top of her voice that Davita jumped.

"Billy! Where are yer? Come 'ere! I wants yer!"

There was no response for a moment. Then just as Mrs. Jenkins opened her mouth to shout again, a strange-looking, under-sized man, with arms that were too long for his body and a leg that limped, came to the door on the other side of the kitchen.

"Wot yer want?" he asked.

"Sleepin' again?" Mrs. Jenkins demanded. " 'Ow often do I have to tell yer, there's work to be done?"

"I were working," Billy answered sullenly.

"Well, work yerself out the door an' find a cab for this young lidy."

Billy looked at Davita with what she thought were bright, rather intelligent eyes which belied his appearance. Then he gave her a grin.

"A'noon, Miss."

"Tell the driver to take 'er to the Gaiety—to the stage-door!"

As Billy passed Davita and started up the stairs ahead of her, Mrs. Jenkins shouted:

"An' mind 'e don't over-charge yer. Ninepence is th' right fare from 'ere to th' Gaiety, an' threepence for th' tip."

"Thank you for telling me," Davita said, and hurried up the stairs after Billy.

The Gaiety was ablaze with lights. Katie had told her that it was the first Theatre in London to have electric lighting, and although it was what Davita had expected, it seemed dazzling.

The stage-door, the cabby told her, was down an alley-way at the side of the Theatre.

Davita expected to see young men in top-hats outside it, but there were only a few poorly dressed people, obviously waiting to see the actors and actresses arrive.

Then she told herself that of course the "Stage-Door Johnnies" would not be there until after the Show.

There were a number of messenger-boys arriving with magnificent baskets and bouquets of flowers, and she followed them nervously through the open door.

Inside, there was what looked like the Ticket-Office in a Railway-Station, and behind the counter was an elderly man with grey hair, surrounded by the flowers for the actresses.

On the walls of the tiny room, which was no bigger than a cupboard, there were pictures of Gaiety Girls and the leading actors and actresses.

Despite the warmth of the evening, there was a fire, and the moment Davita appeared, the old man left it to say politely:

" 'Evening, Miss, an' what can I do for you?"

"Could I please see . . . Miss Violet Lock?" Davita asked.

The elderly man looked at her keenly.

"Is she expecting you?" he enquired.

"I . . . I think so," Davita answered. "She knew I was coming to . . . London from Scotland."

The elderly man raised his eye-brows.

An old sea-captain, Tierney, unlike many stage-door keepers, was always polite and never forgot a message. He knew almost by instinct who could go in and who should not. Davita was not aware of it, but for the moment he could not place her.

She was obviously not one of the girls who were always trying to sneak in and get an autograph or a souvenir from one of the actors they admired, nor did she look as if she wanted a part.

As if she was suddenly aware of his hesitation, Davita said:

"I am a . . . sort of . . . relative of Miss Lock."

Old Tierney smiled.

"Then you'd better go up and see 'er," he said. "Third floor at the top of the First Floor. If she doesn't want you, you're to come back down again. You understand— Miss?"

The "Miss" came after just a slight hesitation, as if Tierney had suddenly decided she was entitled to it.

"Thank you very . . . much," Davita said breathlessly.

Then she was climbing an iron staircase, thinking as she did so that whatever the Theatre was like in the front, at the back it was not very prepossessing.

It was also rather frightening because it was so busy.

As she went up the staircase, several people passed her in a hurry, going either up or down, in various stages of dress and undress which made her want to stare at them curiously.

When she reached a long corridor with doors opening off it, she could hear the chatter of voices and laughter, and when a door opened she had a glimpse of several women in various stages of undress.

She hurried to the door that had been indicated.

She knocked, but because she was nervous it made very little sound.

The voices she heard inside did not stop talking.

Then she knocked again, and this time somebody called out: "Come in!"

She opened the door and found herself facing a long room in which there were a number of women, each, to Davita's startled gaze, more beautiful than the last.

Several were sitting in front of mirrors, applying grease-paint to their faces, two were struggling into very elaborate, brightly coloured gowns, helped by two elderly women.

One at the far end of the room was being laced into a very tight corset, and with a leap of her heart Davita recognised Violet.

She moved forward, and as she did so the woman nearest to her said sharply:

"Shut the door behind you!"

Apologetically, Davita obeyed, and as she did so Violet recognised her.

"Davita!" she cried.

Because there was a warmth in her voice which Davita recognised, she hurried across the room to fling her arms round her.

"I am here, Violet! You were expecting me?"

"I got your letter and I knew you'd turn up sooner or later," Violet said. "I suppose Ma Jenkins sent you here?"

"Yes, she did. And she has given me a room."

"That's all right then."

As Violet spoke, she turned her head to look back at the dresser who was lacing up her corset, and said:

"Here, Jessie, not too tight! I can't breathe!"

"You don't have to!" Jessie answered.

"If I faint on the stage, it'll be your fault, not mine!"

With barely a pause between the words, Violet went on to Davita:

"Let's have a look at you! Goodness, I wish I had a complexion like yours! I suppose you'll say it's all that Scottish air. Well, there's too much of it for my liking!"

"Oh, Violet, you did not mind my coming, did you?" Davita questioned. "I had nowhere else to go, and I have to find employment of some sort."

"You said in your letter your father was dead. Didn't he leave you anything?" Violet enquired. "What about the Castle?"

"It was . . . mortgaged," Davita said in a small voice, feeling embarrassed at talking so intimately when there were other people round her.

But the other women were paying no attention, chatting amongst themselves as they continued to apply cosmetics to their faces or were buttoned into their gowns.

The woman who was dressing Violet now produced the most beautiful dress that Davita could possibly imagine.

It swirled out from her tiny waist in elaborate frills ornamented with roses and bows of silk ribbon.

The bodice, however, seemed to Davita almost embarrassingly low, and she thought that if she had to wear such a gown she would feel extremely shy.

Roses decorated the small sleeves and the décolletage, and there were roses, tulle, and feathers on the magnificent hat which the dresser was setting in place on Violet's fair, elaborately arranged hair.

She sat down on a chair in front of the mirror to put it on, and Davita exclaimed:

"How lovely you look, Violet! I am not surprised that people flock to the Theatre to see you."

"And a few others," Violet said, "but wait 'til you see the Show!"

"I would love to do that," Davita answered. "Do you think it would be possible for me to get a seat in the Gallery, or somewhere cheap?"

Violet looked at her as if she were joking. Then she
said:

"I'm not having that! Not when you've come all the
way from Scotland to see me!"

She thought for a moment. Then she said:

"I know. I'll put you in the Box with Bertie. He ought
to be here by now."

"No, no. Please do not trouble," Davita said quickly.
"I do not want to be a nuisance to anybody. Perhaps I
can wait here until you are ready to leave."

Violet laughed as if she had made a joke.

"If you're suggesting that when I leave here I'll be
going straight home, then that's where you're wrong,
Miss Innocent!"

She looked at the dresser who was arranging her hair.

"We don't go home after the Show, do we, Jessie?"

"Might be better if yer did occasionally!" Jessie answered tartly. "All these late nights'll make yer old before yer years, yer mark my words!"

Violet laughed spontaneously, just as she had when
she had been in Scotland with Davita.

"I've got a bit of time left to get my 'beauty-sleep,' as
you call it," she answered, "when nobody asks me out to
supper."

As she spoke, Davita realised that she had been very
stupid.

She had somehow thought that when she stayed with
Violet they would be together and she would go back
with her to her lodgings.

Now she knew that, looking so lovely, Violet would
have a "Stage-Door Johnny" waiting to take her to the
places her father had mentioned—Romano's or Rules—
and there would certainly be no point in her waiting.

"I am sorry, Violet," she said quickly. "I did not mean
to be a bother coming here. I will go back and we can
talk tomorrow."

"You'll do no such thing!" Violet said.

She turned her face first one way, then the other, looking at her reflection in the mirror. Then she said:

"That's all right, Jessie. Now nip down and find out if Lord Mundesley's in his usual Box, and if he is, ask him to come through the stage-door and speak to me for a moment."

"The Guv'nor don't like gentlemen coming through 'fore the interval!" Jessie said.

"I know he doesn't," Violet replied, "but I've got to introduce His Lordship to my friend, haven't I? Go on, Jessie, and hurry up!"

Jessie flounced off with rather a bad grace and Davita said anxiously:

"Oh, please, Violet, I shall be all right. I can see the Show another night."

"What's the point of waiting?" Violet asked. "Let's have a look at you."

She turned round from contemplating her own reflection to look at Davita.

"Your gown's not bad," she said. "It's a bit dowdy, and it's not right for the evening, but you'll pass."

Her eyes rose a little higher and she said:

"I remember that hat. What have you done with the feathers?"

"It was so kind of your mother to give it to me," Davita said apologetically, "but it looked rather overpowering on me."

"She owed you something, didn't she," Violet said with a touch of humour in her voice, "nipping off like that. Your father must have been a bit upset."

Davita drew in her breath, remembering how dreadfully upset her father had been; in fact, after he'd lost Katie he'd been incapable to cope with life at all.

"Yes, he minded very much," she said in a low voice.

"I'm sorry," Violet said casually, "but after all, she'd

never have stuck all that empty space for long. I had a letter from her—it must be three months ago—and she was doing all right."

"On Broadway?" Davita asked curiously.

"No, she was on tour," Violet replied. "I gather she'd left Harry for someone else."

For a moment Davita was too shocked to reply.

It seemed bad enough that Katie should have left her father to go to America with another man, but that she should have already left him seemed both incredible and positively wicked.

Then Davita told herself that she had no right to judge anybody, and she was honest enough to know that Violet was right. Katie could never have stayed in Scotland for long, especially when there had been no money to buy her all the pretty things that she expected.

"Do you really mean you've got no money?" Violet asked suddenly.

"Very little," Davita replied. "My father's Solicitors suggested they might get me a job looking after children in Edinburgh, but I thought I could find something I would like better in London."

"With your looks, you don't want to be cluttering yourself up with other people's children!" Violet said scathingly.

Then she smiled.

"You leave it to me, Davita. I'll look after you and see you have a bit of fun for a change!"

She put out her hand in a slightly protective manner to pat Davita on the arm.

"You gave me a good time when I came to Scotland," she said, "and I'll do the same for you."

There was a sudden rat-tat on the door and a boy's voice called:

"Ten minutes, lidies!"

Violet rose from the chair.

"Where's that Jessie?" she asked.

As she spoke, the dresser came wending her way through the other women towards her.

"You've given him the message?" Violet asked.

"Yus, but yer'll have to hurry if yer're going to see 'im."

"I know! I know!" Violet replied. "Come on, Davita!"

She walked across the room like a ship in full sail and Davita followed her.

They went down the iron staircase, which now seemed even more crowded with people than it had been before.

They greeted Violet admiringly or jokingly.

Then when they reached the Ground Floor, Davita heard Violet speak to somebody and saw that standing just in front of the door that obviously led into the Auditorium was a man in evening-dress.

He looked, she thought at first, very magnificent with his stiff white shirt and tail-coat, a tall, shiny top-hat on the side of his head.

Then at a second glance she realised that he was older than she had expected. He had heavy moustaches and side-whiskers, and his figure had thickened as if he was approaching middle-age.

However, Davita could see that he was a gentleman, and the voice in which he spoke was cultured, which was made all the more obvious because Violet's voice was, Davita had noticed before, at times slightly common.

"Hullo, Bertie!"

"You sent for me, my fair enchantress," Lord Mundesley replied, "and of course to hear is to obey!"

"I haven't got much time," Violet said quickly, "but this is the daughter of my Stepfather, if you can work that out, and she's just arrived from Scotland and wants to see the Show. She's never been in London before, so look after her for me—and no tricks!"

"I do not know what you mean!" Bertie said in affronted dignity which was obviously assumed.

Then he swept his silk hat from his head and put out
his hand.

"How do you do? Perhaps the alluring Violet will introduce us a little more elegantly."

"I expect you'll introduce yourself, Bertie!" Violet
said. "This is Davita Kilcraig, whose father was the Baronet my mother married."

"And left!" Lord Mundesley added.

"All right, so she left him," Violet retorted, "but that's
none o' your business and it wasn't Davita's fault neither!"

"Of course not," Lord Mundesley agreed.

He was still holding Davita's hand, which made her
feel a little embarrassed.

He was about to say something when a boy's strident
voice called: "Three minutes, lidies!" and Violet gave a
little cry.

"See you after the Show!" she said, and picking up her
skirts with both hands ran back up the staircase.

"We had better go to the front of the house," Lord
Mundesley said to Davita.

He opened a door for her, and, because he obviously
expected it, Davita preceded him down some steps and
found herself in the Auditorium of the Theatre.

The noise of the audience seemed to hit her almost
like a wave, then there was a kaleidoscope of colour,
and, as women passed her being shown to their seats in
the Stalls, the fragrance of exotic perfumes.

"This way," Lord Mundesley directed.

Davita climbed a small staircase which was very different from the iron one behind the scenes. The walls
were painted in an attractive colour, it was lit with electric light, and there was a thick carpet under her feet.

A moment later she found herself in a Box draped with
red velvet curtains and with seats covered in red plush.

Lord Mundesley seated her on his right so that she
had the best view of the stage, and he sat in the centre of

the Box, picking up a pair of Opera-glasses which rested
on the ledge.

Davita stared about her with an excitement that made
it impossible to speak.

She had several times been to a Theatre in Edinburgh,
but it had been nothing like as large and certainly not as
colourful as the scene before her now.

Everything seemed to sparkle, and the crimson and
gold of the Boxes, the splendour of the dropped curtain,
and the lights were only part of the background for the
audience.

Never had she imagined it possible to see so many
attractive, beautiful women and distinguished-looking
men congregated together in one place.

Then, as she was staring almost open-mouthed at the
people being packed into the Stalls, at the Royal Circle
filled without an empty seat to be had, and the Gallery
sloping up to the ceiling and apparently just as full, the
lights were dimmed.

The Orchestra that had been playing softly swelled in
a crescendo until the sound seemed to vibrate through
the whole Theatre and become part, Davita thought, of
her very breathing.

Then she forgot everything except the excitement of
seeing for the first time in her life a Show at the Gaiety.

Because she had of course been interested in what was
being produced at the Theatre in which first her Stepmother had played, and then Violet, she knew that the
Show she was about to see was called *Cinder-Ellen
Up-Too-Late*.

The Lead had originally been played by Nellie Farren,
one of the great stars of the Gaiety, but now she had left
because she had rheumatic trouble which made it impossible for her to carry on.

The few newspapers that Davita had read in Scotland
which reported what was happening in London had all
declared what a tragedy it was for the Gaiety that one of

the greatest Leading Ladies they had ever known should
have been forced to retire.

Hector, who had often seen Nellie when he was in
London with her father, had told her with what for him
had been fulsome praise of her achievements and her
courage.

"Her wouldn'a gi' in wi'out a struggle," he had said to
Davita, "an' it'll be awful hard for 'em to find someone to
replace her."

"I would like to have seen her," Davita had said, thinking it was something she would never be able to do any
more than she would ever see the Gaiety itself.

Yet here she was, watching a new edition of the Show,
and she was aware that Lottie Collins, who had been in
the Gaiety chorus and was the well-known skipping-rope
dancer, had now taken over the Lead.

It was difficult, however, to think of anything but the
beauty of the stage-sets and the dancing of the *corps de
ballet*.

And of course there was the elegance of Violet and the
seven other girls like her as they came onto the stage,
looking so exquisitely beautiful that she thought that every man in the Theatre must fall in love with them.

Just once when Violet was on the stage, Davita glanced
at Lord Mundesley sitting next to her and found, to her
surprise, that he was looking not at Violet but at her.

She wanted to tell him how much she was enjoying
herself, but she thought she should not speak, and instead gave him a shy little smile.

Then her eyes went back to the stage.

There was an amazing performance from Fred Leslie,
and Davita was to learn later that he was a unique draw
of the Show.

Then after several dancing-sequences and some very
comic performances, Lottie Collins came onto the stage
dressed in a red gown and a big Gainsborough hat, with
her blonde hair streaming over her shoulders.

She sang softly, almost timidly, it seemed to Davita, making a great play with a lace handkerchief.

She sang the verse of a song in the manner, although Davita did not know it, of a Leading Lady in a Light Opera, quietly, simply, and perhaps rather nervously:

> "A smart and stylish girl you see,
> The Belle of High Society,
> Fond of fun as fond could be—
> When it's on the strict Q.T.
> Not too young, and not too old,
> Not too timid, not too bold,
> But just the very thing I'm told,
> That in your arms you'd like to hold . . ."

Then suddenly, so suddenly that Davita started, the chorus crashed out, wildly, boldly, and noisily, and the first boom was accompanied by the bang of drums and a terrific crash of cymbals which seemed almost to break the ear-drums.

Then, with one hand on her hip, the other waving her handkerchief, Lottie appeared to go mad.

Her voice and those of the chorus seemed to grow louder and louder:

> "Ta-ra-ra-boom-de-ay,
> Ta-ra-ra-boom-de-ay,
> Ta-ra-ra-boom-de-ay,
> Ta-ra-ra-boom-de-ay!"

The whole Theatre was filled with it, and as her hair streamed the hat bobbed, her short skirts whirled and showed her white petticoats. She was primeval, Bacchic, with all the fury of wild abandon that was associated with a Gypsy dance.

As Davita found it difficult to breathe and impossible even to think, and she could only stare in astonishment, the refrain grew wilder and wilder and the drums, the cymbals, and the wild dancing swept the audience off their feet.

There was a last *"Ta-ra-ra-boom-de-ay"* that finished with the whole audience shouting and applauding, the gentlemen shouting "Bravo! Bravo!" while those in the Gallery were screaming their heads off.

It was not what Davita had expected. It was not anything she could have imagined in her wildest dreams would occur at the Gaiety.

Only as the curtain fell and the applause gradually subsided did she look at the man sitting next to her. His eyes were still on her face and he was smiling as if at her surprise.

Because she felt he was waiting for her to speak, she said in a hesitating little voice:

"I . . . I had no idea . . . that . . . anyone could . . . dance like that."

"Were you shocked?"

"N-not . . . really."

"I think you were," he said with a smile. "Lottie is rather overwhelming when she lets herself go."

"How . . . how can she do that . . . every night?" Davita enquired.

Lord Mundesley gave a laugh.

"That is what acting is all about. Come, let us go and see Violet. We are allowed to go behind during the interval."

He led the way and they had to push through crowds of people moving from their seats and also a number of men who were walking in the same direction as themselves through the small door which led behind the scenes.

It took them some time to climb the staircase, and now in the dressing-room the eight girls who shared it were already holding Court.

Davita noticed there were dozens more bouquets than

there had been before the performance began, and each beautiful Gaiety Girl, looking more attractive than the last, was receiving her admirers.

Violet was already talking to two gentlemen when Lord Mundesley and Davita joined her.

"What did you think of the Show?" Violet asked Davita.

Because she did not reply, Lord Mundesley answered for her.

"She was stunned and a little shocked!"

"Shocked?" Violet questioned. "Well, I suppose Lottie would seem a bit of a firebrand to anyone who'd just come off the moors!"

"Of course! Your friend is Scottish!" one of the gentlemen ejaculated. "I should have known it, with that colour hair."

"It's not out of a dye-bottle, if that's what you're insinuating!" Violet said sharply.

"I would never be so ungallant as to suggest anything of the sort!" the gentleman replied.

"I want to talk to Miss Violet alone," Lord Mundesley said in a proprietary manner which made the two gentlemen who were there before him move off to speak to the other girls.

"Bertie, you're being bossy, and I don't like it," Violet complained.

"I only want to ask you if Miss Kilcraig is coming to supper with us," Lord Mundesley said. "In which case, I will have to find somebody to partner her."

"No . . . no, please," Davita said quickly in an embarrassed tone. "You have already been kind enough to let me share your Box, but as soon as the Show is over I will go back to my lodgings."

"There is no reason for you to do that," Lord Mundesley replied. "In fact, I think as this is your first night in London it would be a great mistake. Do you not agree, Violet?"

Davita thought uncomfortably that Violet hesitated moment before she said:

"Of course! I want Davita to come with us. She's staying with me, isn't she?"

"Very well," Lord Mundesley said. "Shall I ask Tony or Willie?"

Violet glanced at him provocatively, Davita thought, from under her dark, mascaraed eye-lashes before she said:

"How about the Marquis?"

The expression on Lord Mundesley's face changed.

"Do not mention that man to me!"

"I heard his horse had beaten yours today."

"Damn him! That is the third time, and it has made me hate him even more than I did before!"

There was something ferocious in the way Lord Mundesley spoke, and it seemed to Davita to be almost as violent, though in a different way, as the dance she had just witnessed.

Violet laughed.

"Why waste time hating him? He always seems to get the better of you!"

"You are deliberately trying to make me lose my temper!" Lord Mundesley said aggressively. "You know what I feel about Vange."

"Well, for Heaven's sake, don't tell me," Violet said. "I've listened to Rosie crying her eyes out all the afternoon."

"Are you telling me he has broken off with her?" Lord Mundesley enquired.

"Chucked her out, bag and baggage, from his house in Chelsea, and told her she was lucky to be able to keep the jewellery."

"He is intolerable!" Lord Mundesley ejaculated. "I loathe him, and a great many other people feel the same."

"Rosie for one!" Violet said. "But it's her own fault for

losing her heart. I told her what he was like when they first started."

"You were not the only one," Lord Mundesley said. "Rosie is a silly little fool, but one day I will see that Vange gets his just deserts. Then we will see who has the last laugh!"

Davita knew by the expression on Violet's face that she was about to make some mischievous reply, when there was a knock on the door and the call-boy's voice chanting:

"Ten minutes, ladies! Ten minutes!"

There were cries from all the women, and the men moved towards the door.

Before they had even reached it, the dressers were undoing the elaborate gowns at the back and a change of clothing had begun.

Davita gave Violet a smile before she hurriedly followed Lord Mundesley out of the dressing-room and into the corridor, and only as they reached the Box again did she say to him:

"Please . . . Lord Mundesley . . . let me go back to my lodgings afterwards . . . I do not want to be a . . . nuisance."

"You are certainly not that," Lord Mundesley said, bending towards her, "and quite frankly, Davita—and I hope I may call you that—I find it entrancing to watch you experience for the first time the delights of London."

He paused before he added softly:

"And there are many more delights I want to show you!"

There was something in the way he spoke which made Davita feel shy.

She was not quite certain why, but she thought perhaps it was because he seemed so old, experienced, and worldly-wise, while she was exactly the opposite.

He was obviously Violet's "young man," if that

was the right term, and because she had no wish to
talk about herself, she asked:

"Who is the gentleman who has made you so cross?"

"The Marquis of Vange!" Lord Mundesley answered.
"A most unpleasant character, and a man you must
studiously avoid."

"In what way is he so wicked?" Davita asked.

Lord Mundesley smiled.

"That is the right adjective to describe him, and
make no mistake, Davita, he is the villain in a plot
which is unfolding before your young, innocent eyes!
There is, of course, also a hero, and I hope you will
realise, my pretty little Scot, that that is the part I
wish to play."

Davita stared at Lord Mundesley incredulously, feeling she must have misunderstood what he said.

Then as once again the expression in his eyes made
her feel extremely embarrassed, it was a relief when
the lights went down and the curtain rose.

Chapter Three

Davita looked about her with a feeling of excitement.
'So this,' she thought, 'is Romano's!'

It was not very far from the Theatre, and, as she
had expected from all her father and Katie had told
her, the moment they were bowed into the Restaurant by a dark, suave little man who was Romano
himself, the atmosphere seemed to be filled with
laughter.

It was an oblong room with dark red draped curtains and plush sofas, and most of the tables were
already filled with women who, like Violet, appeared
overwhelmingly beautiful.

The décolletages of their gowns were extremely low, their
waists so small that a man's two hands could easily meet
round them, and they were as colourful as the flowers
that decked their tables.

Suspended over some tables were blossoms fashioned
like bells which bore the names of famous actresses.

Lord Mundesley was shown to a table for four, and
Davita and Violet sat on the comfortable sofa while
the two men sat opposite them.

Davita realised that Violet was not important enough
to have her name on a flower-bell, but she could see
one on which was emblazoned "Lottie Collins," and
two others with "Linda Verner" and "Ethel Blenheim,"

who were also stars in *Cinder-Ellen Up-Too-Late*.

Everything was so glamorous that Davita told herself she looked a positive country mouse beside the other women, and a Scottish one at that.

At the same time, she was thrilled at the chance of seeing Romano's and was glad that after so much anticipation she was not disappointed.

People were arriving all the time, and while Lord Mundesley ordered supper, a bottle of champagne in an ice-bucket was brought to their table immediately.

Davita looked round wide-eyed, hoping that if she never had the chance of coming here again, she would always remember what it looked like.

The fourth member of the party was a fair-haired young man who, she thought as they were driving there in Lord Mundesley's very comfortable carriage, seemed rather stupid.

However, she learnt he was the son of a Duke and his name was Lord William Tetherington.

He was obviously very enamoured of Violet and never took his eyes from her as she sat opposite him.

The next table was empty and it remained so until they had almost finished their meal.

Then as Lord Mundesley lit a cigar and sipped a glass of brandy, Romano escorted a tall, dark man to the empty table.

He was alone and therefore sat down on the sofa to look round him in what Davita thought was a somewhat contemptuous way, as if he thought the place was not good enough for him.

At the same time, he was extremely good-looking, and he had an air of authority which Davita somehow expected an important English gentleman would show, even though she had seen very few of them.

Then she realised that while she was staring at the newcomer, Lord Mundesley had stiffened and there was a frown between his eye-brows.

He had been very genial until then, making them laugh and paying Violet extravagant compliments, though at the same time Davita realised he was continually looking at her in a manner which made her feel shy.

Then she heard Lord William say:

"Congratulations, Vange! I thought your horse would win, so I backed it heavily!"

Davita gave a little start.

Now she realised that the newcomer was the Marquis of Vange, whom Lord Mundesley hated so violently and had disparaged several times during supper.

As if the Marquis was suddenly aware of who was at the next table, he replied to Lord William:

"I am afraid you cannot have got a very good price, as it was favourite." Then, turning to Violet, he said: "Good-evening! I was thinking tonight when I watched you on the stage that I have seldom seen you look lovelier!"

"Thank you," Violet replied.

Davita was surprised to see that after all she had said about him, she showed no animosity towards the Marquis, and in fact she gave him her hand and looked at him coquettishly from under her mascaraed eye-lashes.

The Marquis turned towards Lord Mundesley, and, seeing the scowl on his face, he said with a mocking smile:

"I suppose, Mundesley, you expect me to apologise for beating you by a head?"

"I have my own opinions as to how that was possible," Lord Mundesley replied disagreeably.

"Are you suggesting that either I or my jockey was breaking the rules?" the Marquis enquired.

Now there was a hard note in this voice that was unmistakably a challenge.

As if he realised he had gone too far, Lord Mundesley said quickly:

"No, of course not! I was naturally disappointed."

"Naturally!"

There was no doubt, from the expression on the Marquis's face, that he was well aware of Lord Mundesley's feelings.

Then he saw Davita, and she sensed that in some strange way his eyes took in every detail of her appearance and he was surprised that she was so badly dressed.

A waiter was at his side, waiting for his order, and he turned to take the menu in his hand.

"Damn! He would be sitting next to us!" Lord Mundesley said in a low voice to Violet.

Then, as if he thought he had been indiscreet, he deliberately addressed Lord William in honeyed tones, as if to bridge over the uncomfortable moment.

To Davita it was all rather fascinating and like seeing a play at the Theatre.

As the Marquis sat alone eating his supper and making no effort to speak to them again, it was as if his very presence brought a feeling of constraint to their party.

Violet had just begun to point out some celebrities in the room when an extremely beautiful young woman, whom Davita realised she had seen in the same dressing-room as Violet, crossed the Restaurant to stand beside the Marquis.

For a moment she did not speak. Then as he looked up at her she said:

"I want to talk to you. I *must* talk to you!"

He did not rise to his feet but merely looked up and said quietly but distinctly:

"There is nothing for us to talk about, as you well know."

"I have a lot to say."

She spoke with an hysterical tone in her voice, and Violet bent forward to say to her quietly:

"Please, Rosie, don't be stupid."

Davita realised that this was the Rosie whom Violet had been talking about to Lord Mundesley.

She looked so beautiful that Davita wondered how the Marquis could resist her. But Rosie ignored Violet and said:

"If you won't listen to me, I'm going to kill myself! Do you hear? I'm going to kill myself now—at once! Then perhaps you'll be—sorry!"

As she finished speaking she burst into tears, and as they ran down her pink-and-white cheeks she repeated brokenly:

"I—I'll kill myself—I'll kill—myself!"

Violet jumped up from her seat and put her arms round Rosie, and as she did so she gave Lord Mundesley a frantic glance, imploring him to help.

"You can't make a scene here!" Violet said. "Come on, Rosie dear, it'll be best if you go home."

"I don't—want to go—home," Rosie tried to protest through her sobs.

But with Violet on one side of her and Lord Mundesley on the other there was nothing she could do but let them draw her away from the table towards the door.

Only as they moved away did Lord Mundesley say over his shoulder:

"Order my carriage, will you, Willie?"

Lord William hurried to obey, and Davita was left alone at the table, wondering if she should follow them but feeling that she would only be in the way.

She was staring at their backs as they moved rather slowly towards the door of the Restaurant, since Rosie was obviously resisting being taken away, when the Marquis remarked:

"I suppose I should apologise."

Davita realised he was speaking to her and turned her

head to look at him, her eyes very wide and astonished at what had just taken place.

As if he understood her surprise, he said:

"I can assure you, this is not a usual occurrence at Romano's. I have the idea this is your first visit."

"Yes . . . I only . . . arrived in London . . . tonight."

She thought it would be correct and would show good breeding to speak quite calmly and not to appear upset by what had happened. But her voice sounded very young and breathless.

"Where have you come from?" the Marquis enquired.

"From . . . Scotland."

"Then I can understand that for the moment everything seems strange, but you will get used to it."

He did not sound as though he thought that was a particularly enviable prospect, and Davita, again trying to behave normally, replied:

"I have always heard about . . . Romano's . . . and the . . . Gaiety . . . but they are very much more . . . exciting than I . . . ever imagined they would . . . be."

"That, of course, is a matter of opinion," the Marquis said cynically. "They are certainly the best that London can provide."

He spoke as if other countries could do better, and Davita felt that if he disparaged both the Theatre and the Restaurant, it would somehow spoil it for her. So she asked:

"Have you had a great deal of . . . success with your horses this . . . season?"

"I have been lucky," the Marquis replied. "You sound as if you are interested in racing."

Davita smiled.

"I am afraid I have never seen an important race, only those that take place in Edinburgh, and the Steeple-Chases which my father sometimes . . . arranged when he had a good horse."

As she spoke, she thought that the Marquis would

certainly think this was not particularly interesting, and she added quickly:

"But I think a Thoroughbred is the most beautiful animal in the world!"

"I agree with you there," the Marquis said, "and from the way you speak, I presume you enjoy riding."

"Whenever I have the chance," Davita answered. "My father considered me a good rider, although of course he may have been prejudiced."

"One could hardly blame him for that."

As the Marquis spoke, Davita thought that he looked her over in the way a man might take in the good points of a horse. His eyes seemed to linger for a moment on her hair. Then he said:

"I see your escorts are returning, in which case I will bid you good-night, and hope that you will be sensible enough to return to Scotland as quickly as you can!"

He rose to his feet as he spoke, and Davita was so surprised by what he had said that she could find no words with which to reply.

The Marquis moved away to speak to somebody on the other side of the Restaurant as Violet sat down beside her and Lord Mundesley took the seat opposite.

Davita realised that Lord William was not with them, and, as if she had asked the question aloud, Violet said:

"Willie's taking Rosie home."

"I could have done that," Davita said quickly. "Why did you not send for me?"

"She'll be all right with Willie," Violet replied, and Lord Mundesley added:

"We have no wish to lose you, my pretty little red-haired Scot!"

There was a note in his voice and a look in his eyes which now made Davita feel not only uncomfortable but that in some way she was being disloyal to Violet.

"As we are now three," Lord Mundesley said, "there is room for me to sit between you, which will be much more comfortable, and I shall also be extremely proud to be a thorn between two such exquisite roses!"

Once again Davita felt as if she were taking part in a Theatrical performance and that Lord Mundesley was over-acting.

When he sat between her and Violet she felt as if he encroached on her, and although she tried to squeeze herself away from him, she was very conscious of his closeness.

Once or twice, as if to emphasize what he was saying, he put his hand on her knee and she could feel his fingers through the thin silk of her gown.

It was a relief when Lord William returned.

When he did, he sat down in a chair opposite them and said before anyone could speak:

"I want a drink—and a strong one! I must say, Violet, you make me do some damned uncomfortable things!"

"Is she all right?" Violet asked.

"I left her with Gladys, who lodges in the same building, and she said she would look after her."

"I thought Gladys was away," Violet said, "or I'd have suggested it myself."

"She has just returned," Lord William replied, "but I gather she will not be staying for long. I think Sheffield intends to marry her."

Violet gave a cry of delight.

"Do you mean that? Oh, I *am* glad! It'll be wonderful for Gladys if she pulls that off!"

"Do not count your chickens," Lord Mundesley interrupted. "Sheffield's father will cut him off with the proverbial shilling if he marries an actress."

"If that's true, it's extremely unfair!" Violet said hotly. "After all, Belle married the Earl of Clancarty and they're happy enough."

"After some ups and downs!" Lord Mundesley said.

"Every marriage has them!" Violet snapped. "What we've got to do is to find Rosie a nice husband."

"I can assure you it will not be Vange," Lord William said.

"He's behaved abominably," Violet exclaimed, "but then, he always does!"

"I know what you feel about Vange," Lord William replied, "but if you ask me, he should not have got involved with her in the first place. I know Rosie is beautiful, but the way she went on in the carriage when I was taking her home made me think she is a little unhinged."

"She is a bit hysterical," Violet agreed.

"Well, I cannot see Vange putting up with that sort of thing, and what is more, women, however beautiful, never look their best when they are crying."

"You are quite right," Lord Mundesley agreed. "I like a woman to laugh."

As he spoke, he turned his head to look at Davita and said:

"I expect a great many people have told you that you have a laugh like the chime of silver bells, or perhaps like a little song-bird."

"Nobody has told me that before," Davita replied with a smile, "but I am glad you do not think my laugh is like the sound of a grouse flying down the hill, or like the noise the gulls make when they come in from the sea in bad weather."

"I assure you that everything about you is entrancing!" Lord Mundesley said in a low voice.

Davita felt his knee pressing against hers.

On the drive home, which was very late—in fact it was the early hours of the morning—she found it hard to stay awake.

They did not have a long way to go, but Lord Mundesley insisted on sitting between her and Violet on the back-seat, and to her consternation he put his arms round both of them and said:

"Now, my sweet girls, tell me if you enjoyed this evening and how soon we can repeat it."

"I reckon we ought to take Rosie out with us next time," Violet replied.

Davita had the idea that it was not something she really wanted but was an excuse to exclude herself.

Then she thought that perhaps she was being over-sensitive, but she had noticed a cold note in Violet's voice when they had gone to the cloak-room so that she could collect her wrap before they had left the Restaurant.

"It has been a wonderful, wonderful evening!" Davita had exclaimed.

"I'm glad you've enjoyed yourself," Violet had replied, "but you don't want to believe everything His Lordship tells you."

"No, of course not," Davita had answered, "but it was kind of him to be so polite."

Violet had given her a rather sharp glance and asked:

"Is that what you call it?"

Now as they drove along she suddenly said:

"I've got an idea!"

"What is it?" Lord Mundesley enquired.

"It's a way you can get even with the Marquis, if that's what you want."

"Get even with him?" Lord Mundesley echoed. "I want to knock him down—annihilate him! I would shoot him, if it were not for the thought of facing the hang-man."

"Then listen to me . . ." Violet began.

She put her arm round Lord Mundesley's neck to pull his head down so that she could whisper in his ear.

Davita knew she must not listen, so she bent forward, trying to free herself from Lord Mundesley's arm round her waist, and said to Lord William:

"There are so many things I want to see while I am in London that I do not know where to begin."

"I will show you some of them with pleasure," Lord William replied.

"I did not mean that," Davita said quickly. "I was just thinking that it would be very exciting to go sight-seeing, but first I have to find myself some sort of employment."

"Are you thinking of going on the stage with Violet?" Lord William enquired.

Davita shook her head.

"I knew tonight it would be something I could never do. To begin with, I have no talent, and for another, it would frighten me terribly!"

"All you have to do is to look beautiful, and that should not be difficult," Lord William said.

"I have no intention of going on the stage," Davita said firmly. "There must be other things I can do."

"My mother was saying the other day that there are only two careers open to a lady," Lord William replied, "either to be a Governess or a Companion."

Davita thought that was the same idea that Mr. Stirling had suggested.

"There must be others," she said.

"I expect there are," Lord William said vaguely, "but if you ask me, you would have a far better time if George Edwardes could find a place for you."

Davita felt there was no point in reiterating once again that she had no wish to go on the stage, but before she could speak, Lord Mundesley exclaimed:

"My God, Violet! I believe you have something there! It is certainly an idea!"

"Well, think it over," Violet answered.

As she spoke the horses came to a standstill and Davita saw that they were outside Mrs. Jenkins's tall, dingy house.

"Good-night, Bertie," Violet said to Lord Mundesley, "and thanks! You're always the perfect host, as you well know."

"Good-night, my dear. I will be in touch with you tomorrow, and I will have a word with Boris. He's the man we want for this."

56 *Barbara Cartland*

"Yes, of course. The Marquis would never refuse one of the Prince's parties," Violet replied.

So they were back talking once again about the Marquis, Davita thought, as she followed Violet out of the carriage, and she had a feeling, although she could not be sure, that they were plotting something against him.

Lord Mundesley kissed Violet good-night in the small, dark hallway, and Lord William also kissed her on the cheek.

"You have been rather unkind to me this evening," Davita heard him say. "Will you have supper with me tomorrow?"

"I'll think about it," Violet replied.

She looked at Lord Mundesley as she spoke, but he was raising Davita's hand to his lips.

"Good-night, and thank you very, very much," she said. "It was the most exciting evening I have ever spent."

She did not wait for his reply because when he had kissed her hand she had been half-afraid that he would try to kiss her cheek, and she knew she had no wish for him to touch her.

She had in fact hated the feeling of his lips on her skin.

As she reached the turn in the stairway she looked back to see that Violet had not followed her but was talking to the two men.

She was speaking in a low voice and very earnestly, and both Lord Mundesley and Lord William were listening to her intently.

Davita could not be sure, but she felt that once again they were talking about the Marquis.

'It is ridiculous for them to hate him so violently!' she thought, and remembered how he had advised her to return to Scotland.

It was none of his business, but she went on thinking of what he had said even when she was in bed, and so tired after such a long day that she expected to fall asleep immediately.

Instead, in the darkness she kept seeing the Marquis's handsome face, his cynical, almost contemptuous expression, and that penetrating look in his eyes.

To her surprise, when he had told her to go back to Scotland she had felt as if he was speaking sincerely and was really thinking it was the best thing for her.

Then she told herself quickly that there must be a very good reason for Lord Mundesley and Violet to dislike him so much.

Rosie obviously loved him, and he must have done something to make her fall in love with him so frantically.

Thinking back, Davita remembered Violet saying that the Marquis had turned her out "bag and baggage."

She wondered what that meant and why he should have done such a thing.

Had she been staying with him as his guest? And what had Violet meant when she said the Marquis had remarked that she was lucky to be able to keep the jewellery?

Davita remembered her mother saying that no lady accepted presents from a gentleman unless she was engaged to marry him.

It was then that she understood.

Of course! The Marquis must have asked Rosie to marry him, then perhaps because they had quarrelled the engagement had been broken off.

That was why Violet had said they must find her a husband, and Lord Mundesley had said sarcastically that the one person who would not marry her would be Vange.

It struck Davita that Rosie must have been very stupid to have lost the Marquis once he had asked her to be his wife.

She was well aware that because actresses had such a

bad reputation it was unusual for them to marry into the aristocracy.

But it had happened, as when her father had married Katie King, and, as Violet had mentioned this evening, another Gaiety Girl, Belle Bilston, had married Lord Dunlo, who afterwards had become the Earl of Clancarty.

Katie had told her that they lived in Ireland and had twin sons, and she had laughed when she said it.

"That's something your father and I aren't likely to have, so don't worry that you might lose your inheritance."

Davita had assured her at the time that she had not thought of such a thing, and, thinking of it now, she could not help feeling that she would have had a small inheritance indeed if she had had to share the one hundred ninety-nine pounds with twin half-brothers.

Katie had mentioned another Gaiety Girl called Katie Vaughan, who she had said was the biggest star the Gaiety had ever known, and she had married the Honourable Arthur Frederick Wellesley, nephew of the great Duke of Wellington.

"But that marriage," she had said in her gossipy way, "ended upside-down in the Divorce Courts."

'That might have happened to Papa,' Davita thought, 'if he had wanted to re-marry after Katie had left him.'

Instead he had just taken to drink, and she wondered if the Gaiety Girls did in fact make such very good wives.

She was just dropping off to sleep when it seemed she could almost hear the Marquis's voice saying:

"Go back to Scotland!"

* * *

The next morning Davita awoke at what seemed to her to be a disgracefully late hour, and she sat up staring at the clock beside her bed incredulously to find it was a quarter-to-ten.

'Violet will think I am very lazy,' she thought.

Then she knew she was being foolish because Violet certainly would not yet be awake.

However, she washed herself in the cold water that was in a china ewer in the corner of her tiny room, extracted a day-gown from her trunk, and went downstairs to the kitchen.

Mrs. Jenkins, with her hair in curling-rags, was cooking on the range.

"Good-morning, Mrs. Jenkins," Davita said.

"I suppose you're looking for breakfast," Mrs. Jenkins replied. "Well, yer're a bit early, but I'll see wot I can do."

"Early!" Davita exclaimed.

Mrs. Jenkins laughed.

"Those as come 'ere from the country all starts by appearing at the crack o' dawn. Then they soon gets into the Theatre ways. Yer'll find yer friend Violet won't open her blue eyes 'til after noon, and then only if she's lunching with one o' the 'Nobs.' "

"I would love some breakfast, if it is no trouble," Davita said. "I am hungry."

"Then sit down and I'll fry yer some eggs," Mrs. Jenkins said. "Yer'll find a pot of tea on the stove. There's a cup and saucer in the cupboard."

Davita fetched the cup and saucer, poured the tea out of the brown china pot, and found that it was so strong that it would be impossible to drink it unless she added some hot water.

Fortunately, there was also a kettle boiling with which to dilute what seemed more like stew than ordinary tea, and in a cupboard she found a jug filled with very thin, watery-looking milk.

Because she was genuinely hungry and had drunk very little champagne last night, she ate a hearty breakfast for which she thanked Mrs. Jenkins profusely.

"Don't thank me," the Landlady replied, "yer're payin'

for it, as yer'll find when you gets the bill at the end o'
the week!"

She thought there was a frightened expression in
Davita's eyes, and added kindly:

"Now don't yer fret yerself, child. I'll not over-charge
yer. And one day yer might find yerself in the lead an'
drawing two hundred pounds a week like Lottie Collins."

"Two hundred pounds a week!" Davita exclaimed.

She began to think that perhaps she was being stupid
about not going on the stage. Then she remembered
Lottie Collins's performance, and knew that Lord Mundesley had been right. It had indeed shocked her!

Even though she was acting, for a woman to appear so
abandoned, so out of control, had made her feel ashamed.

She knew in her heart that she wanted to be like her
mother, soft, sweet, feminine, and at the same time intelligent and able to do almost anything well.

That was not to say that riding, fishing, shooting, and
making a house a happy place were accomplishments for
which anyone would employ her.

Then uncomfortably she knew the answer.

What her mother had been was a very accomplished
wife, and Mr. Stirling had been right when he had said
she ought to get married.

'Perhaps I shall meet someone here in London,' she
thought, and knew, although she had no reason for thinking so, that it was unlikely.

She was quite sure that whatever Katie might have
said about Gaiety Girls getting married, the men she had
seen last night were out to enjoy themselves and were
not looking for a wife amongst the glamorous, lovely
actresses they escorted to Romano's.

They were fascinated, amused, and certainly entertained by the charmers sitting under the flowery bells
inscribed with their names, or leaning towards them

across the table in a manner which made the lowness of their elaborate gowns seemed somewhat immodest. But that did not mean marriage.

"Besides," Davita said to herself, "if I married into that sort of life, I would be like a fish out of water."

As if it was something somebody had said aloud, she knew she would never marry any man unless she loved him.

When Lord Mundesley had put his arm round her she had felt a little shiver of distaste go through her, and when he had kissed her hand good-night she had wanted to snatch it away from him.

Why did she feel like that, when he had been far more affectionate towards Violet and had kissed her on the lips?

Davita shuddered as she thought of how unpleasant it would be to feel his mouth touch hers, and she told herself, although she knew it was very stupid, that she hoped she would never see him again.

'I will have to find out about a Domestic Bureau to-day,' she thought, and said aloud to Mrs. Jenkins:

"Is there a Domestic Bureau near here where employers engage staff?"

Mrs. Jenkins turned from the stove to ask:

"What do yer want a Domestic Bureau for?"

"I have to find myself some work, Mrs. Jenkins."

"Yer mean yer're not planning to go on the stage like yer friend?"

Davita shook her head. Then she said anxiously:

"You would not refuse to keep me because I have said that? I know you only take Theatrical people, but I am very happy here with you."

"Don't fret yerself," Mrs. Jenkins replied. "I'll not turn yer away. I can see yer're a lidy without knowing who yer father was. But wot sort of work was yer planning on gettin'?"

"I really do not know," Davita replied. "It is . . . difficult. I have no experience and everything I have been taught seems particularly unsaleable."

She thought Mrs. Jenkins looked at her in a rather strange way before she replied:

"Perhaps Violet'll 'ave some ideas on the subject. She can look after 'erself, that one can!"

"She is so beautiful," Davita said. "I can understand her getting good parts in the Theatre, even if she does not act."

Mrs. Jenkins did not reply but returned to her cooking, and Davita went on as if following the train of her thoughts:

'Perhaps she will get married . . .'

She stopped as she thought she had been very stupid.

Of course Violet would marry Lord Mundesley!

She had made it very clear that he belonged to her, and he certainly had behaved in a very possessive manner. Why otherwise should she have kissed him?

"You see, Mrs. Jenkins," she said, "if Violet gets married, then I should have to find someone else to be with, and . . ."

"What makes yer think she's likely to be married?" Mrs. Jenkins interrupted.

"I was thinking that perhaps she is secretly engaged, although she has . . . not told me so, to Lord Mundesley."

Mrs. Jenkins gave a short laugh without much humour in it.

"Now yer're barking up the wrong tree," she said. " 'Ow d'yer expect Violet to marry Lord Mundesley, when he's married already!"

* * *

Later that day, when she was shopping with Violet, who was ordering herself a new gown and a hat to go with it, Davita told herself that she had been very stupid.

It had never struck her for one moment that Lord

Mundesley, and perhaps a great number of other men amongst those she had seen last night, were enjoying themselves without the company of their wives.

She supposed she was ignorant in such matters because her father and mother had always been so happy together, and it had never entered her head that there could be anyone else in their lives.

Her first feeling had been one of indignation that Lord Mundesley should behave as he did, kissing Violet and flattering her when she had a wife all the time.

Then she felt very lost and ignorant and even more afraid of the glittering world in which she found herself than she had been before. She wondered if Lord William was a married man, or the Marquis.

But if the Marquis was married he could not have been engaged to Rosie. In which case, why had he invited her to stay in his house in Chelsea, then turned her out?

It all seemed incomprehensible, and although Davita longed to ask Violet a lot of questions, she felt it was impertinent and she might resent it.

So instead she tried to concentrate on the gown which Violet was choosing in what seemed to Davita a large and impressive shop in Regent Street.

Finally when Violet was satisfied that she had found what she wanted, she ordered some alterations to be made and insisted that the dressmaker added more lace and ribbon to the already elaborate dress.

Only when she had finished did Davita ask:

"What are we going to do now?"

"We'll have some tea at Gunters in Berkeley Square," Violet answered, "and while you're enjoying one of the best ice-creams you've ever tasted in your life, I want to talk to you."

She spoke in a mysterious manner which made Davita look at her apprehensively, but she did not say anything as Violet, dressed once again in her own gown, pinned her hat covered in flowers on her fair hair with jewelled hat-pins and picked up her handbag.

"The gown will be ready tomorrow afternoon, Ma'am," the dressmaker promised, "and may I add that it is always a great pleasure to have the privilege of dressing you, Miss Lock."

"Thank you," Violet replied.

"I went to the Gaiety the other night for the fifth time! I thought you looked wonderful, you really did!"

"Thank you."

"Shall I send the gown to the same address?" the dressmaker enquired.

"Yes, please."

"And the bill as usual to Lord Mundesley?"

Violet nodded.

As they walked away, Davita felt as though somebody had struck her a sharp blow on the head.

The person who was paying for the gown was Lord Mundesley, who was a married man, and Davita was certain that the bill would be astronomical.

It was something that would have shocked her mother considerably, and Davita was not quite certain whether she should tell Violet she thought it wrong, or say nothing.

Then she remembered the bills her father had run up, which she had found after he had died.

Of course the gowns and dozens of other things he had ordered had been for Katie, whom he had married, which was a very different thing.

But even that was wrong, for a man to dress a woman before she was actually his wife.

'I wish somebody could explain it to me,' Davita thought unhappily.

Then she told herself it was something that need not concern her, as long as she behaved in a way that she knew was right and of which her mother would have approved.

They drove in a hackney-carriage to Berkeley Square, where on one corner of Hay Hill was a bow-fronted shop filled with small tables.

It was quite early in the afternoon, but there were a number of people already seated, and when Violet had ordered two strawberry ice-creams Davita understood why.

They were more delicious than anything she had ever eaten, and when she said so, Violet smiled at her enthusiasm.

"I thought you'd enjoy them, and now it's time to have a little chat. I want to have a rest before I go to the Theatre, and if we start talking then, I shan't get a chance of some shut-eye."

"What do you want to talk to me about?" Davita asked.

"Yourself," Violet said. "You told me you came here to get some work, and I'd like to know what your father left you."

"Exactly one hundred ninety-nine pounds, ten shillings!" Davita answered. "But out of that I had to pay my fare to London, so it will not last forever."

"You're not carrying it with you?" Violet asked.

"I would not be so stupid as that. I put most of it in the Bank, and I have a cheque-book of my own!"

"A cheque-book's all right," Violet remarked, "but the Bank-balance is nothing to write home about it; it's got to last you to your old age."

"That is what worries me," Davita said, "and now you understand why I have to find something to do, and quickly."

"I don't mind telling you it's what I suspected," Violet said. "Ma always was extravagant and I guessed she'd clean your father out before she left him."

"Why did you think that?" Davita asked.

She had the awful feeling that Violet was about to say: "because she always did," but instead there was an uncomfortable silence until Violet replied:

"I just knew your father wasn't a rich man."

Davita ate a spoonful of the ice-cream before she said in a low voice:

"Everything had to be sold, and all I possess is now in my two trunks."

"I don't suppose that's worth much, judging from the wardrobe I've seen so far," Violet remarked.

Davita flushed.

She was not going to explain that the dress she was wearing had been her mother's.

She knew only too well how dowdy it must appear to Violet, in her fashionable, expensive clothes which had been paid for by Lord Mundesley.

"Now if you ask me," Violet was saying, "you've as much hope of finding anyone to employ you as flying over the moon. You are too young, for one thing, and for another it'd be just sheer waste of your looks."

Davita stared at her in surprise, and she said almost angrily:

"Come on, Davita! Don't play the idiot with me! You're as aware as I am that with your red hair and your baby-face, most men are ready to fall flat at the sight of you."

"I am sure that is not true."

"It's too true for my liking," Violet said somewhat tartly, "but never mind that. What I want to do is to set you up one way or another, either with marriage, which is difficult, or with money, which is easier."

"What . . . do you mean . . . easy?" Davita enquired.

"I'm not going to say too much now," Violet said, "but I want you to promise to trust me and leave me to look after you."

She paused before she went on:

"I'm fond of you, Davita. You know as much about life as a chicken that's just popped out of the egg. But as there's no-one else, it's got to be me!"

"I do not wish to be a nuisance to you."

"I know that," Violet answered, "but it's my duty to see that you aren't reduced to the same state as Rosie."

Davita stiffened.

"I hope I never behave in such an uncontrolled manner," she said, "but I was very, very sorry for her."

"She only had herself to blame," Violet replied. "She's the whining, complaining, possessive sort, which would bore any man after he'd got used to her face."

Davita thought that was rather hard, but she said nothing, and Violet went on:

"Now, you're different. That young spring-like look would charm the wisest old pigeon off the tree. But if it's my pigeon, it's something I've got to prevent."

"I do not . . . understand."

"That's all the better!" Violet replied. "What you've got to do is promise me that whatever happens, you'll do what I tell you and say nothing I wouldn't want you to say in front of other people."

Davita continued to look puzzled and Violet went on:

"What I'm asking you to do is to believe that I'm doing everything in my power that's in your best interests. Is that clear?"

"Y-yes . . . of course . . . I am very grateful," Davita answered. "It is just that I do not . . . understand . . ."

"You don't have to," Violet said.

She put up her hand to call the waiter.

"Come on, I must go home now or I'll look hideous, and we are going to a party."

"A party?" Davita exclaimed.

"Yes, a really good one given by a friend of mine, and you'll enjoy it. Have you got a decent evening-gown?"

"I do not know what you would think of it," Davita answered.

"What's wrong with it?"

"Nothing . . . it is . . . white."

"White?"

"It was my mother's wedding-gown, which she altered and sometimes wore on special occasions."

"Well, that's exactly what you want," Violet exclaimed. "A wedding-gown. It couldn't be more suitable!"

Chapter Four

They drove back to their lodgings, and while Davita was longing to ask Violet a hundred questions, she had the feeling that she would not answer them.

At the same time, she was very touched that Violet should be so concerned for her.

After all, she was well aware that she was somewhat of an encumbrance, and she told herself that she must try to find a job on her own and not impose on Violet.

'She is right,' Davita thought, 'I am ignorant of the world, but how could I be anything else after living in Scotland and seeing so few people?'

Of one thing she was determined—she would not be critical of Violet or her friends.

It was nothing to do with her if Violet liked to be friends with a married man, and even less her concern that they should hate the Marquis and plot against him.

When she thought of last night, it seemed to her a whirligig of colour, noise, and laughter. At the same time, the Show itself had been an excitement which she felt she would always remember.

The glamorous actresses, the beauty of the girls like Violet, and the laughter evoked by Fred Lacey were all like something out of a dream.

"Goodness, I'm tired!" Violet said suddenly, breaking in on her thoughts. "It's all these late nights. Thank goodness I can get nearly two hours' sleep before we have to go to the Theatre."

"Am I to come with you?" Davita asked.

"Of course you are!" Violet said. "You can sit in the dressing-room—or, if you wish, in the Box with Bertie."

There was just a pause before the last few words, and Davita said quickly:

"I will sit in the dressing-room. After all, I saw the Show last night."

She thought Violet seemed relieved, and she certainly smiled before she said:

"You're a sensible girl, Davita. The trouble is, you're not only pretty but something new, and there's not a man alive who doesn't like a novelty."

Davita looked at her in surprise, not understanding what she was talking about, but because she wanted to please Violet she said:

"I am so grateful to you for being so kind to me. If you had sent me away last night, I do not know what I should have done."

"Leave everything to me," Violet said in a brisk tone. "I've said I'll look after you and I will."

The cab drew up outside their lodgings, Violet paid the cabby, and Billy opened the door to them to say with a grin:

"There be some flowers oopstairs for yer. No guesses who sent 'em!"

"I've told you before not to read the cards on my flowers," Violet said sharply.

"Oi didn't 'ave to," Billy answered. " 'Is Nibs sent 'is footlicker wi' 'em!"

He spoke as if he was glad to score off Violet, but she merely tossed her head as if he were beneath her notice and went up the stairs.

Davita followed her and Violet opened the door of her bedroom, which was a large, well-decorated room at least six times the size of Davita's.

Inside there was a basket of purple orchids that made her exclaim with astonishment:

"I have never seen anything so exotic!"

There were several other floral arrangements in the room, which Davita could not help thinking looked very different from the rest of the house.

The large bed had a pink satin cover on it trimmed with lace which matched the pillow-cases, and there were a number of satin cushions on the *chaise-longue* and on two comfortable arm-chairs arranged on either side of the fireplace.

There were white fur rugs on the floor, and the tas-selled pink silk curtains were very different from the roughly made Holland ones which covered the windows of Davita's room.

What made it different from any other bedroom Davita had ever seen were the photographs which were arranged on the mantelshelf, the dressing-table, and on every other piece of furniture.

Stuck on the wall on each side of the mantelpiece were press-cuttings.

These of course all referred to Violet, and the photographs were mostly of her, although some of them were of other actresses, and one or two of men.

They were all signed, and Davita thought she would enjoy looking at them when there was time.

But Violet said now:

"Undo my gown for me, and the quicker I can get between the sheets, the better. I forgot to tell Billy to knock on my door at five-thirty. Will you remind him?"

"Yes, of course I will," Davita replied as she undid Violet's gown.

She hung it up in the wardrobe, and by the time she had put away her hat, Violet had covered her hair with a net to keep it tidy, slipped into her nightgown, and was in bed.

Davita drew the curtains and as she left the room she fancied that Violet was already asleep.

She thought she would go into her own room and take off her bonnet.

Then when she opened the door she had a shock, for perched on top of one of her trunks, because there was nowhere else to put it, was a basket nearly as large as the one in Violet's room, but instead of orchids it was filled with white roses and lilies.

She was staring at it in astonishment, thinking it must really have been meant for Violet, until seeing the card attached to the handle she pulled it off and read:

To a very bonny lassie from a most admiring
Mundesley

Davita drew in her breath.

It struck her that Violet would be annoyed at Lord Mundesley spending so much money and paying so much attention to her.

She looked at the card, read it again, and wished it was possible to send the flowers back without Violet being aware that he had given them to her.

'I shall have to thank him,' she thought, and she wished again, as she had last night, that she need not see him again.

Then she remembered Violet's message and hurried down the stairs to find Billy.

She reached the last flight and saw him speaking to somebody at the front door. As she came down into the Hall, she could see that it was a servant in livery.

Billy turned round and saw her.

"Ah, t'ere y' are, Miss. Oi were comin' to find yer."

"I was coming to find you," Davita replied. "Miss Lock says please remember to knock on her foor at five-thirty."

"Oi'll not forget," Billy answered. "An' t'ere's some-un 'ere as wants t' speak t' yer."

"Speak to me?" Davita questioned in surprise.

She saw that the servant was no longer standing in the doorway but was outside in the street where there was a closed brougham.

"Who is it?" she asked.

"Oi were just told 'twas a gent'man as wants to 'ave a word wiv yer."

Davita stood irresolute.

It would only be one of two gentlemen, and if it was Lord Mundesley she had no wish to speak to him.

Yet she knew it would be rude to refuse, and it flashed through her mind that while she must thank him for the flowers, she would ask him not to send her any more.

Billy was holding the door open for her, and she walked down the steps and across the pavement to where a footman was standing with his hand on the carriage-door.

When she reached it he opened it, and Davita could see, as she had feared, Lord Mundesley sitting inside.

He bent forward and held out his hand.

"Get in, Davita. I want to speak to you."

"I was just . . . going to . . . lie down."

"I will not keep you long."

Because she did not know what else she could do, Davita put her hand in his to let him draw her into the carriage. As she sat down beside him, the horses started to move and she asked:

"Where are you taking me? I really have to go back."

"We are merely moving a little farther up the road so that we can talk without being observed," Lord Mundesley replied.

She knew without his putting it into words that what he meant was so that Violet would not see them.

He was looking very smart with a carnation in his button-hole and a large pearl tie-pin in his cravat. He also seemed large and overpowering, and the way he was looking at her made Davita feel shy.

Because she was nervous she said quickly:

"I must . . . thank you. It was very kind of you to send me those . . . beautiful flowers. At the same time, I want to ask you . . . not to send me any . . . more."

She thought he might ask her why, but instead he said:

"Are you afraid Violet will be jealous? That is something I wish to talk to you about."

As she spoke, the horses came to a standstill. Davita now realised he had been truthful when he had said they would only go a little way up the street, and she asked more calmly:

"What do you want to talk to me about?"

"The answer to that is quite simple," Lord Mundesley said. "You, and of course myself."

Davita looked at him in surprise and he said:

"You must be aware, my lovely little Scot, that you captivated me from the moment I set eyes on you, and I have a proposition to make."

"A . . . p-proposition?" Davita stammered.

Although Lord Mundesley had not moved while he was speaking, she felt, as she had last night, that he was encroaching on her and instinctively she moved as far as she could away from him to the farther corner of the carriage.

Even so, he still seemed unpleasantly near.

"I understand from Violet," Lord Mundesley went on, "that you have come to London in search of employment. Although I could quite easily arrange for George Edwardes to find you a place at the Gaiety, I do not think you are really suited for a life on the stage."

Davita gave a little sigh of relief, thinking her apprehension had been quite unnecessary and Lord Mundesley was in fact trying to help her in a practical manner.

She turned her face to him eagerly.

"I am so glad you said that, because not only am I quite certain that I would be a failure if I went on the stage, but it is not the sort of life I would like, and Mama would have disapproved."

"Your mother is dead," Lord Mundesley said, "so whether she approves or disapproves of what you do is not likely to concern us."

Davita was puzzled.

She did not understand why he should say such a thing.

"At the same time," Lord Mundesley continued, "your mother would, I am sure, not wish you to endure a life of hardship or have none of the luxuries and comforts to which anybody as pretty as you is entitled."

He paused, and as Davita did not speak he went on:

"What I want to suggest to you, Davita, is that you let me look after you. You will find me a kind and generous man, and I think we could be very happy together."

Davita's eyes opened so wide that they seemed to fill her whole face. Then she asked in a voice that was barely audible:

"What are you . . . suggesting . . . what are you . . . s-saying?"

"I am saying, my dear, that I will give you a comfortable little house in Chelsea, all the beautiful gowns you want, and a great number of other things that will make you happy."

For a moment Davita found it hard to breathe, for she was so shocked and horrified at what he had suggested.

Then as she opened her lips to speak, Lord Mundesley put out his arms and drew her against him.

At his touch she started to struggle violently.

"No! No!" she cried. "How can you think of . . . anything so wrong . . . so wicked? You are a . . . married man, and what you are . . . suggesting is a . . . sin against your wife . . . and God."

She was so vehement that now it was Lord Mundesley's turn to be surprised.

He still had his arm round her, but there was an

astonished expression on his face as she tried to push
him away from her.

"Now listen to me, Davita..." he began, but with a
sound that was almost a scream Davita interrupted:

"I will not... listen! Let me... go! I do not... want to
hear any... more!"

She twisted herself from him, bent forward to open
the carriage-door, and sprang out into the road, so intent
on escaping that she did not realise that Lord Mundesley
was making no effort to stop her.

Then she was running down the pavement towards
the door of her lodgings, and when she got there she
found to her relief that the door was open as Billy was
just taking in a parcel that had arrived from a tradesman.

Davita ran past Billy and pounded up the stairs as if all
the devils of hell were at her heels.

When she reached her own room on the Second Floor,
she rushed in, slammed the door behind her, locked it,
and, edging her way round her trunks, threw herself
down on the bed.

"How... dare... he? How... dare he... suggest such
a... thing!" she panted.

Her heart was beating suffocatingly, and as she ran
away from Lord Mundesley her bonnet had fallen from
her head and was suspended by the ribbons which had
been tied under her chin.

She flung her bonnet on the floor and lay face-
downwards, her face in the pillow.

So that was how men behaved in London! Now she
understood not only what Lord Mundesley was suggesting
to her, but what had happened to Rosie.

How could she have known, how could she have guessed,
that Rosie had been the Marquis's mistress and he had
thrown her out "bag and baggage" not because they were
engaged to be married but because she was a woman for
whom he had no further use.

It was so shocking, so degrading, and Davita had never imagined she would come in contact with anything so evil.

She had vaguely known that there were women who in the words of the Bible "committed adultery" and to whom nobody respectable would speak.

There had been a girl in the village who had run away with a Piper who was married and could not marry her.

Davita had heard the servants talking about her, and when she asked her mother what had happened, she had explained gently and carefully that the girl had lost the love and respect of her parents and of everybody else.

"Why should she do such a thing, Mama?" Davita had asked.

"Because she was tempted," her mother had replied.

"I do not understand," Davita had protested, "why she should want to be with a man who cannot marry her."

"These things happen, dearest." her mother had said, "but I do not want you to think about it now. It is something which is best forgotten."

But because the servants had not forgotten and had gone on talking about Jeannie, it had been impossible for Davita not to be curious.

"I always knew she would come to no good," she could hear them saying to one another. "She'll rue the day she trusted a man who'd throw her aside when he's had all he wants of her."

Davita wondered what he had wanted, but she knew if she asked questions nobody would explain.

She heard two years later that Jeannie had had a baby and, having been deserted by the Piper, had drowned herself and the child.

It was then that she had exclaimed to her mother:

"How could such a terrible thing happen? And why did Jeannie not come home?"

"If she had, they would not have let her in," her mother had replied.

"So you mean that her father and mother would have let her starve?"

"It is something I would never be able to do myself," her mother had admitted, "but I know Jeannie's parents. They are respected members of the Kirk and very strait-laced. They would never forgive their daughter for bringing disgrace upon them."

Davita tried to understand. At the same time, because Jeannie had been young and attractive, she felt it was a terrible thing that she should kill herself and her baby and that no-one should be sorry that she had done so.

Now she thought with a kind of terror that that might happen to her.

How could a gentleman like Lord Mundesley suggest that he should give her a house in Chelsea, and that while he had a wife somewhere else, she should live with him and be his mistress?

It was a degradation she had never imagined for one moment would ever be suggested to her, and she thought how shocked her father and mother would be if they knew.

She was sure that her father, if he were alive, would be prepared to knock Lord Mundesley down because he had insulted her.

Then suddenly she stiffened as she thought of the way Lord Mundesley had spoken to Violet and how he had kissed her good-night.

Could it be possible that Violet was already his mistress?

Then she told herself with a feeling of relief that the answer to that idea was "no."

If she was, Violet would not be living here but in Chelsea, and although he might have suggested it to her, Violet had obviously refused.

The feeling of relief was like a warm wave sweeping through Davita and clearing away the feeling of shock.

Violet was a good girl. Violet would not, Davita was sure, contemplate anything so wicked.

Then why had Lord Mundesley suggested such a thing to her after knowing her for such a short time?

She could not understand, except perhaps that Violet, intending to be kind, had painted such a bleak picture of her future with no money and no job that he had made the suggestion because in his own way he wanted to be kind.

Davita could still feel his arms pulling her against him, and she had the feeling that if she had not struggled, he might have kissed her.

"I hate him!" she said aloud, and knew there was something unpleasant about him that was difficult to put into words.

'I shall never see him again!' she thought.

Then she knew that she would have to do so if she went to the party tonight.

"I will stay here. I will stay at home," she decided firmly, and got up from the bed to pick up her bonnet and put it tidily away.

Then as she did so she realised that if she told Violet she was not going to the party with her as they had planned, she would have to give a very good explanation as to why she had changed her mind.

What could she say that would not upset Violet?

It was obvious, although she had not said so, that Violet thought Lord Mundesley was her admirer and in a way her property.

Looking back, Davita could remember dozens of little words and gestures that proclaimed all too clearly that Lord Mundesley had devoted himself to Violet.

Now, disloyal and unfaithful—although that was hardly the right description considering that he was married—he was ready to transfer his affections to her.

'I cannot tell Violet that!' Davita thought in a panic. 'It

would upset her, and she has been so kind to me.'

She looked round the tiny room, feeling as if the walls whirled round her as she tried to think what she could say and what she could do.

Then she knew, almost as if somebody was saying it aloud, that it would be extremely unkind if she let Violet know what had happened.

'Sooner or later she will find out for herself what he is like,' Davita thought, 'but I must not be the person to tell her so.'

She sat down on her bed and tried to think clearly and she sent up a prayer to her mother for help.

"I am in a mess, Mama," she said. "Tell me what I should do. Tell me how I can avoid Lord Mundesley without hurting Violet, who has been kind . . . very, very kind."

She almost expected to hear her mother answer, and gradually a plan came to her mind.

She would have to go to the party tonight rather than make Violet suspicious, and she was quite sure that Lord Mundesley would not tell Violet what he had suggested.

Tomorrow, first thing, she would go to a Domestic Bureau and take a job, any job that she was offered.

Davita gave a little sigh.

"I am sure that is the right thing to do," she told herself.

It was reassuring to think that if her first job was an unpleasant one, she had enough money to support herself while she waited for another.

The idea that she would be alone and frightened came insidiously into her mind, but she swept it aside.

The only thing that mattered now was to get away from Lord Mundesley.

"Once I am gone, he will think only of Violet again, and if I do not give her my address there will be no chance of his trying to get in touch with me," Davita decided.

To her surprise, she found herself wishing she could ask the Marquis to advise her. She had thought of him during the night and how handsome he had looked despite his cynical and contemptuous air.

He had told her to go back to Scotland, and he had been right: that was what she ought to do.

Perhaps he had guessed that Lord Mundesley or some other man like him would make such horrible suggestions to her simply because she was with the Gaiety Girls.

"He was right, absolutely right. I should not be here," Davita said to herself.

Because she was upset and still shocked by what had happened, when a little later she went to do up Violet's gown before they went to the Theatre, the latter exclaimed:

"You look very pale, Davita! It must be your gown, but I should have thought white would have suited you with your red hair."

"I think I am just a little tired," Davita replied. "Is this gown all right?"

Violet turned to look at her.

"It's really rather pretty in its own way."

Davita herself had always thought it very lovely.

It was made of Brussels lace and her mother had always told her that because it had come from the best shop in Edinburgh, it had caused a sensation at home in the Western Isles when she had worn it to marry Sir Iain Kilcraig.

"They had never seen anything like it, Davita," she had said with a smile, "and neither had I. My Godmother gave it to me because she was so pleased I was marrying such a distinguished man, and when it arrived a week before my marriage, people came from all over the island to look at it!"

"You must have looked lovely on your wedding-day, Mama," Davita had remarked.

"If I looked lovely it was not because of the gown," her

mother had answered, "but because I was so happy. I
loved your father, Davita, and he was and is the most
handsome man I have ever known."

The lace had a fragility about it, and to Davita it had an
almost fairy-like loveliness that made her feel like a Prin-
cess in a fairy-story.

It was the first time she had had the opportunity of
wearing it, and she felt, because it revealed her neck and
white shoulders, that for the first time she was really
grown-up.

"I must behave as though I am," she admonished herself, "and not allow Lord Mundesley to upset me!"

It was an easy thing to say, but when after the Show
was over she followed Violet downstairs to where he was
waiting at the stage-door to escort them to his carriage,
she felt a quiver of fear inside her and knew it was impossible to look at him.

Lord Mundesley, however, was completely at his ease.

"Violet, you look more adorable than usual!" he said as
he kissed her hand.

"Why didn't you come round at the interval, Bertie?"
Violet asked.

"I had some friends to see," Lord Mundesley replied,
"and although they wanted to meet you, I wished to
keep you to myself."

The way he spoke made Davita think he was deliberately warning her that he was ready to reassure Violet
that he belonged to her if she had by any chance tried to
make trouble.

She longed to tell him that she would not lower herself
to do anything so unkind or spiteful, but she knew that
the only dignified way to behave was to ignore what had
happened, and she therefore said nothing.

As they drove away from the Theatre, Lord Mundesley
made no effort to sit between them as he had the night
before, but sat on the seat opposite.

Nevertheless, Davita, without even looking in his direction, was aware that his eyes were on her face and she turned deliberately to look out the window.

"Everything's arranged, is it?" Violet asked.

"You can be sure of that," Lord Mundesley replied, "and Boris thought it a huge joke, as I thought he would."

"You are sure that 'You-Know-Who' will turn up?"

"I am sure of it. He intends to discuss the sale of a couple of horses with Boris, and they are bound to have a somewhat spirited argument over the price."

Violet gave a little laugh.

"Horses are always more irresistible than a woman!"

"But not where I am concerned," Lord Mundesley said with a caressing note in his voice. "You look very beautiful tonight. That gown certainly becomes you."

"I'm glad you like it," Violet replied. "I bought it especially for you."

'And he paid for it!' Davita added in her mind, but told herself it was vulgar even to think such things.

She wished she were not going to the party. She wished almost wildly that she were back in Scotland.

Then she told herself with a sudden pride that she would not let Lord Mundesley's infamy defeat or depress her.

This was an adventure, and only if things became too unbearable would she surrender to the inevitable and return to Scotland.

"Davita's wearing her mother's wedding-dress," Violet said unexpectedly.

Lord Mundesley gave a short laugh.

"If there is one thing I love about you, Violet, it is your sense of humour."

"But it's true!" Violet objected.

Lord Mundesley laughed again and Davita thought he was laughing at her mother, and hated him more violently than she had before.

She wished there was a way in which she could warn Violet that he was a man to be avoided.

"Here we are!" Violet exclaimed a little while later. "I can't understand how the Prince when he comes to London always manages to rent the largest and finest houses."

"He managed it because he can afford it," Lord Mundesley answered. "He is paying an enormous rent for this house which he has taken over for the Season. In fact, the Duke said the offer was so astronomical that he could not afford to refuse."

"Well, quite frankly," Violet said, "I'm looking forward to seeing the inside of Uxminster House. All the Duke would be likely to offer me is the outside of his front door!"

Lord Mundesley laughed.

"That is true enough. Uxminster is a dull old fossil. No Gaiety Girls for him!"

"Well, thank goodness the Prince is different!" Violet said as the carriage-door was opened and she stepped out into a blaze of light.

Uxminster House was certainly very impressive as they walked up a red-carpeted staircase to the First Floor, and Davita was glad that she had come after all.

This was the sort of house she had always hoped she would see in London, with family portraits and tapestries on the walls, and huge crystal chandeliers sparkling in the light of hundreds of candles.

To her surprise, they were not shown by a very smartly liveried servant into a room on the First Floor which she could see through an open door was large and extremely impressive.

Instead, they were taken along a corridor and shown at the end of it into a smaller room where they were greeted by their host.

The Prince was a middle-aged Russian, distinguished, bearded, with twinkling dark eyes, and as Davita looked about her it seemed to her almost as if she were back in Romano's again.

The room was massed with flowers, but far more glamorous than any blossoms were the guests, some of whom she recognised as having come from the Gaiety as she and Violet had.

Lottie Collins was there and several other Leading Actresses, all flashing with jewels and wearing gowns that were as spectacular as those that they had worn on stage.

As the evening wore on, Leading Ladies from other Theatres, many of whose names Davita recognised, although not their faces, arrived for the party.

Champagne was being handed round, and about twenty minutes after they had arrived they went into a Dining-Room which led off the room in which they had been received and which was arranged like a Restaurant.

There was a table in the centre, at which the Prince sat with a dozen of his guests, and in addition there were small tables for six, four, and even two. The only light was from the candles on the tables, which gave the room an air of mystery.

At the same time, there was an atmosphere of irrepressible gaiety enhanced by the music.

There were two Bands: one played dreamy, romantic waltzes; the other, a Gypsy Orchestra, wild, passionate, exciting, made the heart beat to the clash of the cymbals and the throb of the drums.

To Davita it was very exciting, and as the Prince introduced her not to one young man but to half-a-dozen, she thought what an excellent host he was, and how because she was never without a partner it was easy to keep away from Lord Mundesley.

In fact, he made no effort to talk to her either intimately or otherwise, but devoted himself to Violet, and when the dancing started he apparently had no wish to leave her for anybody else.

Supper was over before the curtains at one end of the Dining-Room were drawn back to reveal a Dance-Floor.

Those who wished to do so could continue to sit at

their tables, drinking or eating, but still could get up and dance as it suited them.

To Davita's delight, the men to whom the Prince had introduced her were only too eager to ask her to dance with them.

Up until now, although she had had dancing-lessons occasionally in Edinburgh, because her mother had said it was essential that she should be a good dancer, she had danced at home only with her father.

Now for the first time she was able to dance with not one young man but a dozen, and she found it an exhilarating experience.

"You are as light as thistledown," one told her as she was swept round the room to the strains of a Strauss waltz.

It was so thrilling that she forgot her fears about Lord Mundesley, and it was only when she was being whirled round the floor by a tall young man who she learnt was in the Brigade of Guards that she saw the Marquis seated at a table beside her host.

She had not seen him arrive, and she was quite certain he had not been there at supper.

But now, looking as usual cynical and contemptuous of everybody round him, he was beside the Prince, a glass of brandy in one hand and a cigar in the other.

As she looked at him she found that he was looking at her, and she felt that in some way he had mesmerised her into being aware of him.

She almost missed a step, then heard her partner say:

"You have not given me an answer to my question."

"I am sorry," Davita replied. "What was it you asked me?"

"Who are you thinking about?" her partner enquired. "Whoever it is, it is not me."

"I am sorry," Davita said again.

He smiled at her, saying:

"I forgive you. How could I do anything else when you look so lovely?"

Davita did not feel either shy or embarrassed as she had when Lord Mundesley had paid her compliments.

Then once again she was glancing across the room at the Marquis and wondering why Violet and Lord Mundesley had been so keen for him to come to the party when they hated him so much.

"This is my night of gaiety," she told herself.

About two hours later, as she waltzed round the room Davita realised she had not seen Violet and Lord Mundesley for some time.

Then as she looked for them she saw that they were at the far end of the Supper-Room, talking earnestly to the Prince.

'What are they plotting?' Davita wondered.

She was sure that if it was against the Marquis, he would not be affected by it because he was far stronger than they were! Then she wondered what she meant by that.

The dance came to an end and the Prince rose to his feet.

"I have something to say to you," he said in his deep voice with just a slight foreign accent, which made it sound very attractive.

The ladies all flocked towards him, looking as they moved in their full frilled skirts like the flowers that decorated the room.

"What is it, Your Highness?" one of them asked. "Have you a surprise for us?"

"Several, as it happens," the Prince replied. "For one, there is a Cotillion when you will all get very attractive prizes."

There was a cry of delight at this, and one woman said effusively:

"Darling Boris! You are always so generous!"

"I think we both are, Dolores, in one way or another!" the Prince replied. There was a shriek of laughter at the repartee and Dolores laughed too.

"Before the Cotillion," the Prince said, "as it is my birthday, we must have a little celebration."

"Your *birthday!*"

There were shrieks from everyone.

"Why did you not tell us?" "Why did we not know?" "We would have brought you a present!"

"All I need as a present is that you are all here," the Prince replied. "I intend to cut my cake, then you shall drink my health in a very special wine that comes from my own vineyard in my own country."

As he spoke, servants came in carrying an enormous iced cake on which flared a number of candles.

They set it down on a small table in front of the Prince, and as they did so Davita felt her hand taken by Violet.

"Let us get near so that we see," she said.

She pulled Davita through the guests until they stood at the Prince's side.

"I want my friend from Scotland to see this ceremony, Your Highness," Violet said to him. "Everything's new and exciting to her and this is something she mustn't miss!"

"Of course not," the Prince answered, "and I hope, Miss Kilcraig, you will wish me happiness in the future."

"Of course I will!" Davita answered.

The Prince smiled at her, and picking up a knife with a jewelled handle was ready to cut the cake.

"I must blow out the candles first," he said, "and for as many as I extinguish, I shall have as many happy years."

"No cheating!" somebody shouted.

"That is one thing I never do," the Prince replied.

He drew in his breath and with one terrific blow extinguished every candle on the cake.

There were shrieks of delight, then everybody clapped.

"Now wish!" Violet said.

"That is what I am doing, but of course what I wish must be a secret!"

He inserted the jewelled knife into the cake and cut it, then as the servants took it away, others brought huge trays on which there were glasses of wine.

One servant brought a gold tray on which there were only three glasses and presented it to the Prince.

"Now these," the Prince said, "are for myself and my two special guests this evening."

He picked up the glass on the right and, turning to the Marquis, who was at his side, said:

"Vange, you and I have been competitors on the race-course and at times in the race for love. I would like you to drink my health, and may we have many more years ahead of us as competitors and—friends."

"You may be sure of that, Your Highness," the Marquis answered, "and I promise I shall always do my best to defeat you!"

"And I promise I shall strive indefatigably to be victorious!"

There was a roar of laughter at this, then the Prince lifted the left-hand glass and the middle one.

Then to Davita's utter surprise he turned to her and said:

"There is an old superstition in my country that a red-haired woman presents a challenge which all men find irresistible. May I ask you, Miss Kilcraig, as I think you are the only red-headed person present, to drink my health, and I hope that the future will prove a challenge both for me and for yourself!"

Davita took the glass from the Prince's hand and said a little shyly:

"I . . . I hope I may bring Your . . . Highness both a challenge and good luck."

"Thank you."

The Prince raised his glass.

"Let us all drink to the future," he said, "and, in the fashion of my country—no heel-taps!"

Everybody raised their glasses.

"To Boris!" they cried, "and to the future!"

Davita put the glass to her lips, and despite what the Prince had said, she was about only to sip the wine when Violet beside her whispered:

"You must drink it down! Otherwise it's an insult!"

Because she thought that to disobey such an instruction might draw attention to herself, Davita tipped the glass upwards and felt the liquid, which was soft, sweet, and tasted of strawberries, slip down her throat.

She was grateful that it was not the rather harsh, fiery wine she had expected.

Then as she turned her face to look at the Prince, she suddenly felt as if the whole room were moving.

At first it was just a movement like the waves of the sea. Then it seemed to accelerate and whirl as the Gypsy music was whirling, growing wilder and more insistent!

The sound became deafening and with it was a darkness which came up from the floor to cover her. . . .

Chapter Five

Davita realised that her head was aching and she must be very tired.

Her mouth felt dry, and vaguely she wondered if she had drunk too much champagne the night before.

Her eyes felt heavy and seemed to be throbbing, and it was with an effort that she managed to open them.

Then she knew that she must be dreaming, for beside her on the bed, and she thought it was in her lodgings, was a man!

She could see his white shirt and his dark head, and when she shut her eyes to try to make herself wake up, she could feel again the dryness of her mouth and the pain in her head.

Suddenly there were voices and laughter and she opened her eyes to see Violet in the doorway of a strange room and beside her Lord Mundesley.

For a moment their faces swam in front of her eyes, and there was another face too, and she was sure that she was having a nightmare.

Then Violet was saying angrily:

"Really, My Lord! It is disgraceful of you to behave in such a manner to my poor little friend who has only just arrived from Scotland!"

It was then Davita realised that Violet was not looking at her but was speaking to somebody beside her.

Slowly, because she was so frightened that it was almost impossible to move, she turned her head.

The man she had seen in what she thought was a dream was the Marquis!

Now in a horror that made her feel spellbound she was aware that they were lying on a huge canopied bed, with silk curtains falling from a gold corola, side by side on lace-edged pillows.

"I must wake up, I must!" Davita told herself.

But the Marquis did not disappear. He was there in his white shirt without his evening-coat, and he was real . . . real!

As if he was as bemused as she was, he lay very still for a moment. Then slowly he raised himself on the pillow, saying as he did so:

"What the devil is all this about?"

Only when he was sitting up on the bed did he see that Davita was beside him, and as he looked at her Violet said again:

"You have behaved disgracefully! I cannot allow my friend's reputation to be injured, so you will have to make reparation!"

Without saying anything, but with an expression of anger and contempt on his face, the Marquis rose from the bed and Davita felt sure that he was feeling as strange and as hazy as she was.

He picked up his evening-coat, which was lying on a chair, and as he started to put it on Lord Mundesley said:

"It is checkmate, Vange! There are only two things you can do—marry the girl, or pay up."

Davita drew in her breath.

It was gradually percolating through her befuddled mind what had happened. She remembered the toast on the Prince's birthday, and the way she had been forced to drink the whole glass of wine because Violet had said that otherwise it would be an insult.

Suddenly she understood. She had been drugged! She

remembered the room seeming to swing round her before she was overwhelmed by a darkness which rendered her unconscious.

The same thing must have happened to the Marquis, and this was what Violet and Lord Mundesley had been planning: to discredit him, to pay him out for beating Lord Mundesley's horses at the races and for treating Rosie in the way he had.

But why should she be part of the plot?

She knew she must tell the Marquis that it was nothing to do with her.

But because her lips were so dry, although by now she was sitting up, it was impossible either to move or to speak.

She could only watch what was happening, finding it hard to breathe.

The Marquis had put on his evening-coat, and now as he pulled his lapels into place he said in an icy voice:

"Let me make it clear that I will not be blackmailed!"

"I think you might prefer it to being sued for breach of promise," Lord Mundesley said with a sneer.

The Marquis did not reply, and with what Davita felt was an unassailable dignity he started to move towards the door. Then Violet said:

"As Davita is not lucky enough to have any jewellery to keep, I should imagine a sum of—say—five thousand pounds would mend a broken heart."

The Marquis by now had reached the door of the bedroom, and as he went to open it Lord Mundesley said mockingly:

"It is no use, Vange! You are caught—hook, line, and sinker! We have a photograph, in fact several, of you together with this poor, innocent child, and let me point out she is not a Gaiety Girl but respectable and innocent—or rather she was!"

The Marquis walked three paces back to face Lord Mundesley.

The two men confronted each other and Davita saw that the Marquis's fists were clenched and she thought he would strike Lord Mundesley.

With an effort she found her voice.

"N-no . . . please . . . ! This is . . . wrong . . . very wrong . . . I . . ."

Before she could say any more, Violet was beside her.

She caught hold of her arm, digging her fingers into the softness of the flesh as she said in a hissing whisper:

"Be quiet! Don't say anything!"

"B-but . . . I . . ." Davita began, then realised that neither of the men had paid any attention to her interruption.

"I know only too well why you have done this," the Marquis was saying, and his voice was low and controlled.

"You have had it coming for some time, Vange," Lord Mundesley replied. "This time I have slipped under your guard and the only thing you can do is to pay up. As Violet says, it will cost you five thousand pounds to buy the photographs from me."

The way he spoke was even more unpleasant than what he said, and once again Davita knew that the Marquis was considering knocking him down.

Then, as if it was beneath his dignity, he said:

"Go to the devil!"

Then he walked from the room, slamming the door behind him.

For a moment there was silence. Then Violet gave a little cry and asked:

"Have we won?"

"We have!" Lord Mundesley replied. "He will pay up because there is nothing else he can do."

He walked to the end of the bed and, resting his arms on it, leant forward to look at Davita.

"Well, my pretty little Scot," he said, "I have done you a good turn. With five thousand pounds in your pocket, there will be no need for you to go looking for employment for some time!"

As he spoke, Davita was vividly conscious of the look in his eyes, which made her shrink away from him as she had done in his carriage.

She was not only afraid of him, but she hated him so violently that for the moment she was aware only of a disgust which made her feel sick.

Then it swept over her with horror that she had been humiliated and made a participant in Lord Mundesley's and Violet's plot to extract money from the Marquis.

However, some instinct of self-preservation warned her not to say so at this moment, and she merely turned her face towards Violet, saying desperately:

"I . . . want to . . . go . . . home!"

"That is where I'll take you," Violet answered.

She helped Davita off the bed, but when her feet touched the floor she felt as if the room were still swinging round her and she staggered.

"You're all right," Violet said. "You'll soon sleep it off."

She put her arm round Davita's shoulders to lead her towards the door.

"I will help you," Lord Mundesley said.

Davita shrank away from him as Violet said:

"Leave her alone! She's all right. Just see that the coast is clear. She won't want to talk to anybody at the moment."

"Oh . . . no . . . please . . . !"

"Don't worry," Violet said as Lord Mundesley went ahead of them. "Nearly everyone's left by now, and the rest are too drunk to know whether it's Christmas or Easter!"

"What . . . about the . . . Prince?"

Davita vaguely remembered seeing him peering through the door when she first woke up.

"He thinks it's a fine joke!" Violet replied. "He won't

talk, and most of the others didn't realise what had happened. We got you out quick and up the stairs while the rest of the party were toasting their host."

"How . . . could you . . . do such a . . . thing?" Davita asked.

"I'll tell you later."

They reached the stairs and Davita was walking more firmly but she still held on to Violet's arm.

Lord Mundesley's carriage was at the front-door, and as they drove away she leant back and shut her eyes, determined not to talk about it to him.

However, she was obliged to listen to him chuckling and gloating over the Marquis's discomfort in what she knew was a most unpleasant manner.

"I never thought to catch him at such a disadvantage!" Lord Mundesley said in a self-satisfied voice. "Violet, my pet, you are a genius!"

"I'm not worrying about your revenge," Violet replied, "and I couldn't care one way or the other if the Marquis has better horses than you. What I did was to help Davita. She'll be all right now and will need assistance from *no-one* . . ."

There was an accent on the last word that made Davita think Violet was aware of the proposition Lord Mundesley had made to her.

Then she told herself it was impossible, but unless she was blind Violet must have noticed the way he looked at her, which had been very revealing.

'I hate him! I hate him!' she thought, and did not open her eyes until they reached their lodgings.

Then her hatred of Lord Mundesley gave her a burst of energy which enabled her to hurry past him as he assisted first Violet and then herself to alight and be halfway up the staircase before they had reached the hall.

As she turned to climb the second flight, she glanced down to see Lord Mundesley pulling Violet into his arms, and she wondered how she could allow anyone so revolting to kiss her.

It was an inexpressible relief to reach her own bed-room and take off her mother's gown, feeling she had besmirched it and would never wear it again, before Violet came into the room.

"Now don't be upset, Davita," she said in a coaxing tone. "I know it was a bit of a shock, but when you get the Marquis's cheque tomorrow, you'll thank me from the bottom of your heart."

"I will not . . . take his . . . money," Davita said in a low voice.

"Don't be such a little fool!" Violet said sharply. "You know as well as I do you've no alternative, unless you're prepared to accept the suggestion which I suspect Bertie's prepared to make you."

Davita drew in her breath.

"I'm not half-witted," Violet went on. "I know he fancies you, even though he may not have said anything yet."

Davita hoped the relief these last words gave her did not show on her face, and Violet went on:

"Not that I'd mind losing him as much as all that—there's plenty of others! But I know Bertie, and he'd soon tire of you after he got what he wants."

This was the phrase that Davita had heard in her child-hood, and it made her think of Jeannie and how she had killed herself and her baby because the Piper could not marry her.

"How can . . . you be so . . . friendly with him . . . Violet?" she asked. "He is . . . a married man."

Violet laughed.

"I'm not expecting Bertie or any of his kind to marry me," she said, "but he gives me a good time, and he's generous when it comes to gowns and sables. There's a dozen like Willie, bless their hearts, but they haven't got two pennies to rub together."

"But it is . . . wrong," Davita murmured.

Violet gave a little laugh and turned her back.

"Undo my gown, there's a dear, and stop worrying your head over me. I've saved you from being faced with the eternal question of 'starvation or sin,' and that's all that need concern you for the moment."

Davita unbuttoned her gown and Violet with difficulty moved round the tiny room towards the door, saying as she went:

"Good-night, and tell them downstairs that no-one's to wake me 'til I call. I'm dead on my feet!"

As she shut the door behind her, Davita put her hands over her face and sat down on the bed to try and think.

* * *

It was ten o'clock before Davita had finished her packing and asked Billy to carry her trunks downstairs and fetch a hackney-carriage.

She knew that Violet would not wake for at least another two hours, and by that time she would have disappeared.

This was the only thing she could do, for she was certain that however much she protested, however much she swore she would not take the Marquis's money, Violet and Lord Mundesley would compel her to do so.

The mere idea of accepting even a farthing from him was so humiliating that she could almost hear her mother telling her that she must go away and hide rather than be involved in what the Marquis had said so truly was blackmail.

Davita was aware that blackmail was a crime punishable by law, but although the Marquis had been contemptuous of the manner in which he had been tricked, she was quite certain that he would not wish to face a scandal.

"What must he think of me?" she asked. "Does he think I was a parti to what was happening?"

Then she thought despairingly that that was what he must think. Why it should matter to her if the Marquis disapproved of her personally she did not know—but it did!

Because Lord Mundesley was his implacable enemy, Davita was sure that he would not hesitate to allow the photographs that had been taken of them in bed to be printed in the more scurrilous newspapers.

She remembered how her father when he returned from London had brought home a number of newspapers which he told her not to read.

Curious, because they were lying about in his study she had glanced at them, seeing that they were mostly concerned with scandalous stories about the aristocracy and were, she was sure, an effort by the Radicals to discredit the Government and the Conservative Party.

When she thought about it, she realised that if she accepted Lord Mundesley's proposition of installing her in a house in Chelsea, his plot to get at the Marquis would have been dropped.

"But how could he think I could do anything not only so wicked but so . . . disloyal to . . . Violet?" Davita asked herself.

The more she thought about it, the more despicable Lord Mundesley's behaviour appeared.

It was he who had arranged with the Prince that she and the Marquis should be drugged at the party and carried up to the bedroom in his house.

At the same time, because she attracted him, he had been prepared, if she agreed, to call it off at the last moment, drop Violet, and make her his mistress.

It was obvious, Davita thought, that he had not offered Violet a house in Chelsea.

Then she told herself that she was disparaging her friend even by thinking she would sink so low with any man, let alone Lord Mundesley.

Yet Violet accepted expensive gowns from him and, on her own admission, sables.

"I do not . . . understand," Davita complained, and did not want to.

As the night wore on she felt less woolly-headed, more alert, and it was only an hour after she got to bed that dawn broke.

She got up, packed her trunks, and strapped them up as they had been when she arrived from Scotland.

Then she dressed herself in the same garments which had belonged to her mother and in which she had travelled down from the North, and put on the plain but pretty bonnet with the ribbons that tied under her chin.

When she looked at herself in the mirror she saw that there were lines under her eyes and she was very pale.

Otherwise, the horrors of the night appeared to have left little mark on her, although she thought that if her hair had turned white she would not have been surprised.

Then she remembered how before they had drunk the toast to the Prince and he had cut his birthday-cake, the evening had seemed so glorious and exciting.

"My night of gaiety," she told herself, "and I shall never have one again."

She knew that the whole idea of the Gaiety Theatre with its lovely girls were typified by Lottie Collins's dance when she sang: *"Ta-ra-ra-boom-de-ay!"*

First there was her demure appearance in her red gown and Gainsborough hat, and the shy, sweet little verse, before unexpectedly and with a wild abandonment came the chorus.

That was the reality of the Gaiety Theatre and the so-called Gaiety Girls, Davita thought, and the impression they evoked of being refined and ladylike was merely superficial.

"I will never see them or the Theatre again," she told herself, as her hackney-carriage drove away from Mrs. Jenkins's lodging-house.

She had paid for her bed and board, and only when she told her what she owed did Mrs. Jenkins say:

"Violet never tells me yer was leavin' today."

"It was all arranged last night," Davita answered.

"Well, I hopes yer're going some'ere nice, dear," Mrs. Jenkins replied. "With yer face, yer'll have to look after yerself, an' don't forget I told yer so."

"I will remember," Davita replied, "and thank you very much for being so kind to me."

She told the cabman in Mrs. Jenkins's hearing to drive to Waterloo Station, but as soon as they reached the end of the road she put her head out the window, saying she had changed her mind.

"I want to go to the best Domestic Bureau in the West End," she said.

For one moment she was afraid he would say he did not know where there was one, but after a moment he replied:

"Yer means th' un in Mount Street?"

"That is right."

The horse did not hurry itself, and as they journeyed there Davita planned what she would say.

Nevertheless, when they drew up outside the building that had a shop on the Ground Floor with a door at the side of it marked: "*Mrs. Belmont's Domestic Bureau*," her heart was beating in a frightened manner.

She asked the cabman to wait and he grunted a reply. Then she went up some narrow, rather dirty stairs and opened a door on the small landing at the top of them.

Inside there was a narrow room which was exactly what her mother had told her to expect.

On each side of it were long wooden benches on which several servants were seated.

At the far end there was a high desk where there was a strange-looking woman wearing what appeared to be a black wig.

She had a large nose and her thin face was wrinkled

with lines, but her eyes were sharp and shrewd and she
looked at Davita a little uncertainly as she walked up to
her.

As she reached the desk there was a pause before the
woman asked:

"What can I do for you—Ma'am?"

There was a distinct pause before the word "Ma'am,"
and Davita knew she was making up her mind whether
she was an employer or an employee and had come to
the conclusion that she was the former.

"I am looking for a position as a . . . Companion," Davita
replied.

She tried to make her voice sound firm and confident,
but there was a decided tremor on the last word.

Mrs. Belmont's attitude changed immediately.

"A Companion?" she repeated. "Have you any experience?"

"I am afraid not."

"I imagined that was the case," Mrs. Belmont observed
in a hard voice. "And I'd have thought you were far too
young for that sort of position."

Davita had decided in the carriage what she should
say, but it was difficult to speak because she felt Mrs.
Belmont was already dismissing her. However, she managed at length to articulate:

"My mother . . . Lady Kilcraig, when she was . . . alive,
always told me that if ever I . . . needed a position . . . I
should apply . . . to you."

There was a distinct pause.

"Did you say your mother was a Lady of Title?" Mrs.
Belmont enquired.

"Yes. My father was Sir Iain Kilcraig of Kilcraig Castle,
Kirkcudbrightshire, Scotland."

It was obvious that Mrs. Belmont's attitude had changed
once again.

Now she looked at Davita as if she hoped to find something in her appearance to recommend her. Then she

looked down at the huge ledger which stood open on her desk.

Without speaking she turned over several pages.

Then a mousy, middle-aged woman who had been sitting behind her and whom Davita had not noticed before came to Mrs. Belmont's side to whisper in her ear.

Davita heard her say:

"She wants someone immediately and there's no-one else we can send."

Mrs. Belmont turned over another page of the ledger.

"She's too young," she replied out of the side of her mouth.

"But she might fill the gap," the mousy woman replied.

Mrs. Belmont looked at Davita again and made up her mind.

"I've just one place where you might be suitable," she said. "You'd better give me your particulars."

Davita gave her name, but when Mrs. Belmont asked her age she hesitated. Then, fearing that eighteen would sound much too young, she said:

"I am twenty . . . nearly twenty-one."

"You certainly don't look it!" Mrs. Belmont remarked.

"I know," Davita agreed, "but I shall become older in time."

Mrs. Belmont did not smile, she merely noted Davita's age in her ledger.

"Address?" she queried.

"I have only just arrived from Scotland, and I have at the moment no address in London."

"Then you can leave for the country immediately?"

"That is what I should like to do."

"You have your luggage with you?"

"Yes."

Mrs. Belmont had a long conversation with the mousy woman. Then she said:

"Have you enough money to pay your own fare to Oxford?"

"Yes, I have," Davita replied.

"Very well, then," Mrs. Belmont said. "I will send a telegram to say that you are arriving at Oxford on the next train from Paddington. They'll be able to find out which it is and you'll be met at the Station. Your fare will be refunded to you."

"Thank you."

Mrs. Belmont was writing in an untidy, uneducated hand on a card.

It took her some time, and when she had finished she passed it to Davita.

"This is who you're going to as Companion," she said, "and I hope, Miss Kilcraig, you'll do everything in your power to give satisfaction. If you return with a bad reference, it would be very difficult for me to place you in another position. Do you understand?"

"Yes, I understand," Davita answered, "and thank you very much for helping me."

"I don't mind telling you," Mrs. Belmont went on, "that I'm taking a risk in sending anyone so young to the Dowager Countess. She's very particular. In fact, I've supplied her with no less than four Companions this last year, and none of them have settled down or been satisfactory."

"Was it because they wished to leave, or because they were dismissed?" Davita asked.

"I don't think there's any need for me to answer that question," Mrs. Belmont said in a lofty tone. "You just do your best, Miss Kilcraig, and remember that as you're so young and inexperienced, you've a lot to learn."

She held out the card and Davita took it from her.

She looked at it, saw that written on it was *"The Dowager Countess of Sherburn, Sherburn House, Wilbrougham Oxfordshire."*

"Thank you," she said after she had read it. "Thank you very much."

"Now remember what I've said," Mrs. Belmont warned.

"The young never listen to advice, but I expect your mother'd want you to listen to me."

"I will certainly try to please the Countess," Davita promised.

But as she drove towards Paddington Station she was thinking of the four Companions who had failed in the last year to satisfy the Dowager.

Yet nothing mattered for the moment except that she was escaping from Violet, from Lord Mundesley, and from the intolerable position in which they had placed her.

They were not likely to guess where she had gone, and even if Violet was curious enough to make enquiries at various Domestic Bureaus, she would doubtless "let sleeping dogs lie," and be content that she had Lord Mundesley to herself.

"Besides, she will be angry with me for not accepting the Marquis's money," Davita told herself, "and she would never understand why I was not grateful to her for worrying about me."

Violet was willing to accept money and clothes from Lord Mundesley and doubtless from other men, and it would be impossible to explain to her why she could not do the same.

"I am much poorer than Violet, with no salary coming in every week," Davita reasoned. "But she, like her mother, is prepared to take anything anyone will give her. I am different."

She knew that even if she was starving and down to her very last penny, she would not, after what had happened, accept help either from Violet or from Lord Mundesley.

He at any rate would expect a return for his money, and she knew what that was!

'I hate him!' she thought again.

She knew that if it had not been for him, the fairy-like illusion that the Gaiety had brought her the first night she had watched the Show would not have been transformed into something ugly and unpleasant.

Davita could not bear to let her thoughts linger on the moment when she had awakened to find herself lying on the bed with the Marquis.

He was so magnificent that it hurt her to think how he had been treated and how bitterly he would resent it. It would inevitably make him even more cynical and contemptuous than he was already.

"But I will not think about him or the Gaiety or Lord Mundesley any longer!" she told herself.

She tried instead to recall the fairy-stories that had been so much part of her life when she had been in Scotland.

She remembered the tales that her father had related to her of Scottish gallantry, the feuds between the Clans, the superstitions that were so much part of the Highlands.

That was what had been real to her before first Katie and then Violet had come into her life.

She felt now as if they deliberately prevented her from being a happy child and had turned her into a grown-up woman for whom fairy-land could have no reality.

She had a long wait at the Station, and all the time she was trying to think herself back into the happiness and contentment she had known when she walked over the moors, fished in the river, or rode with her father.

Then inevitably when the train carried her nearer and nearer to Oxford she felt apprehensive.

Fortunately, Mrs. Belmont's telegram had reached its destination promptly, for there was someone to meet her at the Station.

As Davita stood feeling alone on the crowded platform, a footman in a smart livery with a crested top-hat looked at her, decided she was not the person he was meeting, and would have walked on if she had not said nervously:

"E-excuse me . . . but are you from . . . Sherburn House?"

"That's right, Ma'am. Can ye be Miss Kilcraig?"

"I am!"

"I've been sent to meet ye," the footman said, "but I were expectin' someone older."

Davita thought with a lowering of her spirits that this was what his mistress also would be expecting.

The footman collected her trunks and made the porter carry them outside the Station to where there was waiting a brake drawn by two horses.

It was too large for one person, but Davita thought perceptively that it was the type of vehicle which would be used to convey servants, and as she climbed into it, she was thankful that for the moment she was the only occupant.

They drove out of the town and were soon in narrow, dusty lanes bordered by high hedges, and Davita looked round her with interest because the countryside was so different from Scotland.

There were small villages with usually in the centre a village green, an ancient Inn, and a duck-pond.

They drove for what seemed a long time before finally the horses turned in through some impressive lodge-gates and started down the long drive.

Now at last Davita had a glimpse ahead of the house and realised it was very large and impressive, although she thought it was not very old and the architecture was decidedly Victorian.

She had always been interested in buildings, and her father had taught her a great deal about those in Edinburgh, including the Castle which overshadowed the city and had always seemed to Davita very romantic.

She had also studied books on English Architecture and she thought now that it was disappointing that she had been in London for so short a time that she had not seen any of the sights.

Even to think of what had happened instead made a little shudder run through her, and the large and impos-

ing mansion which seemed to grow bigger and bigger
the nearer they drew to it seemed a place of safety and
security after her experience of the Gaiety and those
who frequented it.

The brake did not drive up to the front door with its
long flight of stone steps.

Instead, Davita was taken to a side-door which she
told herself with a smile was obviously the right entrance
for anyone of so little importance as a paid Companion.

Here she was met by a liveried footman.

"I suppose ye're th' lady we're expecting?" he said.

"I am," Davita replied, and waited for the inevitable
reaction.

"Ye look too young to be a Companion, Miss. All th'
others had one foot in the grave!"

He obviously intended to be friendly, and Davita
laughed.

"I think it will be a long time before I have that."

"Certainly will. This way, Miss. I'll take ye up to 'er
Ladyship."

He led the way as he spoke up what Davita was sure
was a secondary staircase.

When they reached the landing they turned into a
corridor that was wide and very impressive with high
ceilings painted and gilded.

The furniture was magnificent and so were the paintings,
and Davita hoped that she would have time to see everything in the house before she was dismissed.

'I am obviously going to be much too young,' she thought
despairingly, 'but perhaps I can manage to last a week or
so.'

The footman ahead of her stopped in front of two mas-
sive mahogany doors.

He knocked on one of them and it was opened by an
elderly woman wearing a black gown but with no apron,
and Davita supposed she was a lady's-maid.

"What do you want?" she asked in a rather disagreeable voice.

Then before the footman could reply she saw Davita and said:

"Are you Miss Kilcraig who we're expecting?"

"Yes, I am," Davita replied, wondering how often she would have to answer the same question.

The lady's-maid looked at her critically, but she did not say anything. As the footman walked away, Davita entered a small vestibule with several doors leading out of it.

"Wait here!" the maid commanded.

She went through the centre door and Davita heard her speaking to somebody. Then she opened it, saying:

"Come in! Her Ladyship'll see you."

Feeling as if she were a School-Girl who had been sent for by the Head Mistress, Davita walked into a large room full of light from the afternoon sunshine.

To her surprise, it was a bedroom with a huge four-poster bed against one wall.

Sitting in the centre of it propped up by pillows was an old lady who seemed to Davita quite fantastic in her appearance.

Her white hair was elegantly arranged on top of her head, and beneath it was a face that had once been beautiful but was now lined and very thin.

But what was so extraordinary was the amount of jewellery she wore.

There were ropes of magnificent pearls round her neck, there were diamond ear-rings in her ears, and above her blue-veined hands her slim wrists were weighted down with bracelets.

The bed-cover was of exquisite Venetian lace and she wore a lace dressing-jacket to match it, but it was almost obscured by her jewels.

Davita stood just inside the door.

Then the Dowager Countess said sharply:

"What have they sent me this time? If you are another of those nit-wits who have been popping in and out of here like frightened rabbits, you can go straight back on the next train!"

The way she spoke sounded so funny that Davita instead of being frightened wanted to laugh.

"I hope I will not . . . have to do . . . that," she said.

Then quickly she remembered to add "Ma'am" and to curtsey.

"So you have a voice of your own. That is something!" the old lady said. "Come here, and let me have a look at you."

Davita obeyed, moving closer to the bed.

The Countess stared at her. Then she said:

"You are nothing but a child! How old are you— sixteen?"

"I told Mrs. Belmont at the Domestic Bureau that I was nearly twenty-one," Davita said.

"And how old are you really?"

"Eighteen . . . but I desperately wanted . . . employment."

"Why?"

"For one reason . . . because I wanted to get . . . away from . . . London."

"What has London done to make you feel like that?"

"Things I would rather not . . . speak about, Ma'am," Davita replied, "but I only came . . . South three days ago."

The Countess looked down at something that lay on her lace cover and Davita realised it was a telegram.

"Your name is Kilcraig," she said, "so I suppose you are from Scotland?"

Davita nodded.

"My home was near Selkirk, which is not far from Edinburgh."

"And why did you leave?"

"Both my father and mother are . . . dead."

"And have left you with no money, I suppose?"

Davita did not think it was strange that her whole life story was being extracted from her in a few words.

"That is why I have to find employment," she said. "Oh, please, Ma'am, let me try to do whatever you want. I will make every effort to be satisfactory."

"You are certainly not what I expected," the Countess remarked.

"I can only hope I will not be another . . . rabbit to be sent back on the . . . next train."

"I think that is unlikely," the Countess said. "Now, suppose you let Banks show you to your room, and then you can come back and tell me all about yourself, as I am certain you are anxious to do."

There was something a little sarcastic in the way she spoke, and Davita said quickly:

"I would much . . . rather hear about you, Ma'am, and this enormous . . . exciting house."

"From the way you speak," the Countess said, "I imagine your own home was much smaller."

"It is a crumbling old Castle," Davita replied, "but very, very old."

The Countess laughed.

"I get the implication. Sherburn was built only forty years ago. I suppose that is what you are hinting at."

"I would not have been so . . . impertinent as to . . . hint at it," Davita answered, "but I am glad to think I was not . . . mistaken when I first . . . saw it."

The Dowager put out her hand and picked up a small gold bell that stood on a table beside the bed.

She rang it and the door opened so quickly that Davita suspected Banks had been listening outside.

"Take Miss Kilcraig to her room, Banks," the Countess commanded. "She can come back when she has taken off her travelling-things."

"Very good, M'Lady."

Davita remembered to bob a curtsey before she followed

Banks from the room, and she was almost certain that the Countess smiled at her.

As they walked down the corridor she said to the lady's-maid:

"Please, help me. I would like to stay here, but I am very afraid I shall be too ignorant and inefficient."

Banks looked at her in surprise.

"Most of them thinks they knows everything!"

"I know nothing," Davita replied, "and I am quite prepared to admit it!"

There was just a faint smile on the elderly woman's thin lips.

"Her Ladyship's not easy," she said, "and if you ask me, she doesn't need a Companion. I can do all she wants, if it comes to that."

Davita understood that this was a bone of contention, and she suspected that Banks had had a great deal to do with the Companions being dismissed almost as soon as they arrived.

"I promise you I will not get in your way," she said, "and perhaps I could help you if you would tell me if there is anything you want me to do. I can sew quite well, and I have always pressed my own clothes."

The maid looked at her with what Davita thought was a far more pleasant expression.

At the end of the corridor she opened a door and Davita saw it was a nice bedroom with a high ceiling.

It was well furnished. Already her trunks had been brought upstairs and placed on the floor, and there was a young housemaid starting to unpack them.

"Emily'll help you to unpack," Banks said, "but she's too much to do to give you much attention otherwise."

"I can look after myself," Davita said quickly, "and it is very kind of Emily to help me."

She paused before she added:

"I am afraid there is rather a lot in the trunks. They

contain everything I possess in the world now that
my . . . father is . . . dead."

She could not help there being a little quiver in her
voice on the last words, and Banks asked:

"Has he been gone long?"

"Just over a month," Davita replied. "And my mother
died some years ago."

"You just have to be brave about it," Banks remarked.

Then, as if she felt she was being sentimental, she said
sharply to Emily:

"Now hurry up, Emily. Get everything straight for
Miss Kilcraig."

She would have left the room if Davita had not said:

"One thing I would like to ask . . . although it may seem
rather . . . an imposition."

"What is it?" Banks asked in an uncompromising voice.

"Would it be possible for me to have something to eat?
Just some bread and butter would do. I did not like to
leave the Waiting-Room at Paddington Station before the
train came in, and I have had nothing to eat since breakfast."

"Good gracious! You must be starving!" Banks exclaimed.
"What you want is a cup of tea and something substantial
with it."

"I do not want to be a bother."

"It's no bother," Banks answered. "Nip downstairs,
Emily, and see if you can find something for Miss Kilcraig
to eat. Don't be long about it. Her Ladyship's waiting for
her."

Emily sprang to her feet to do as she was told, and as
she left the room Davita said:

"Thank you very much. You are very kind to me, but I
do not want to be a nuisance and keep asking you for
things."

"You ask," Banks replied. "I'll tell you when you're a
nuisance, and it may be a long time before you are."

She actually smiled before she left the room, and when she had gone Davita went to the window to look out at the view over the Park and the lake.

Then she gave a little exclamation of pleasure.

She had escaped! She was free. She had left Violet, Lord Mundesley, and the Gaiety behind her, and she was here!

Because it was in the country, even though it was very different from Scotland, it seemed like home.

She could see stags moving under the trees in the Park, there were birds flying overhead, and the sun was shining on the lake as it did on the river near the Castle.

It was all so different from London, and she clasped her hands together.

"Oh, please, God, let me stay! Please, God, do not let the Countess send me away."

It was a cry that came from the very depths of her heart.

Then, because she realised time was passing, she hurriedly untied her bonnet and began to take off her travelling-gown.

Chapter Six

Davita shut the book with a snap.

"How could she have died at the end?" she asked, and there were tears in her eyes.

The Countess smiled.

"Most women like a good weep at the end of a story."

"I am sure that isn't true," Davita replied. "I want everyone to live happily ever after."

"I know you do, dear," the Countess said, and her voice was soft. "Perhaps one day you will find happiness."

"I hope so," Davita answered. "Papa and Mama were very happy until she died."

There was a little tremor in her voice because it was always hard for her to speak of her mother, and to think of what had happened when Katie had left her father always upset her.

She did not realise that her eyes were very expressive, and the Countess said quickly:

"Anyway, you have made me happy."

"Have I really?" Davita asked.

"Very happy," the Countess replied. "I feel sometimes that you are the daughter I never had."

Davita gave a little cry of delight.

"You could not say anything which would please me more, because I feel that you are like the Grandmother I never knew. I would have loved to have had a Grand-mother!"

"Then that is what I am quite content to be," the Countess replied.

Davita smiled at her radiantly, but before she could say anything the door opened and Banks came in.

"Now, M'Lady," she said briskly, "time for your rest, as you well know, and Miss Davita should be outside in the sunshine putting roses into her cheeks."

Davita laughed.

"If they were there, I am sure they would clash with my hair."

Banks did not reply but she was obviously suppressing a laugh.

"Before I go out," Davita said to the Countess, "I intend to choose a book in the Library with a happy ending. That is what we both want to listen to."

She did not wait for an answer but hurried from the bedroom.

When she had gone, the Countess began to take off her strings of pearls and said:

"That is a very sweet child, Banks. I am so glad she came here."

"She's one of the nicest young ladies I've ever met, M'Lady," Banks replied. "None of those other complaining women ever offered to help me as Miss Davita does."

Running down the stairs, Davita thought with delight that she had nearly an hour and a half to do all the things she wanted to do.

As soon as she had chosen a book in the Library—she was determined she would not read the Countess an-other unhappy one—she would walk down to the lake, and she wished as she had wished before that her father could watch the trout with her.

'Perhaps one day I might suggest that I fish for them,' she told herself.

Then she decided she would not wish to kill anything, not even a trout.

After that she would go to the stables. She drew in her breath with excitement as she remembered that the Countess had offered to give her a new riding-habit. It should be arriving any day now.

Ever since she had come to Sherburn House three weeks ago, every moment had seemed more thrilling than the last.

Davita sometimes thought it was as if she had come home and Sherburn House belonged to her.

Then she knew she felt this because in her dreams she, or her fanciful heroines who were a part of herself, always had a background which only a grand house could provide.

The paintings, the furnishings, the miniatures, the painted ceilings, and the huge State-Rooms were all part of her dreams, and sometimes she wandered through them pretending that she was in fact a Countess of Sherburn, and the history of the family was her history too.

She had seemed to fit in from the very moment she arrived. Not only did she amuse the Countess, but the servants liked her, and, although she was quite unaware of it, everyone treated her as if she were an entrancing child whom they wished to spoil.

"The Chef has made this pudding especially for you," the Butler would say at luncheon or dinner.

The housemaids would tidy her room and press her dresses and the grooms would keep carrots and apples ready in the stables for her to give to the horses.

"I am so happy," Davita would say to herself when she went to bed.

In her prayers she would thank God not only that she was happy but that she was safe.

"No-one can find me here," she would say reassuringly

to herself, almost every hour during the first week after she arrived.

Then, because there were so many new things to occupy her mind, she began to forget abut Violet and Lord Mundesley and even the Gaiety.

In retrospect it became a dream that had ended in a nightmare, and even her thoughts shied away from recalling the terrible night when she came out of a drugged sleep to find the Marquis on the bed beside her.

The Library of Sherburn House was very impressive, most of the volumes being old and very valuable.

But the Countess's eldest son, to whom the house belonged, had collected quite a large number of modern books when he was at home, and Davita felt grateful to him for affording her such a choice.

The Countess had had two sons, one of whom had been killed fighting in what she described as "one of Queen Victoria's little wars."

The elder, the Earl of Sherburn, was now Governor of Khartoum in the Sudan. Because he was so often abroad, having been Governor in other places before this appointment, he had persuaded his mother to live at Sherburn House and "keep it warm" for him.

"The servants have all been with us for years," she told Davita. "We really would not know what to do with them if my son closed the house, and quite frankly I am happy to live in what was my home for so many years."

"It is a very lovely home," Davita replied, "even though it is a modern building."

"Built onto an ancient foundation," the Countess said sharply.

Her eyes were twinkling because the age of Sherburn House was a joke between her and Davita.

Now Davita ran to the far end of the Library where the modern books had been neatly arranged and catalogued by the Curator.

She took one down from a shelf and put it back again. Then she pulled out another one by Jane Austen, wondering if it would amuse the Countess or if she already knew it too well.

She was turning over the pages when she heard someone come into the Library and thought it must be Mr. Anstruther, the Curator.

She was just going to ask him if the Countess had read *Pride and Prejudice* recently, when she looked round and was suddenly rigid.

It was not Mr. Anstruther who was walking slowly from the doorway towards the mantelpiece, but the Marquis!

For a moment she thought he could not be real and she was imagining him, because he looked just as handsome, imperious, and cynical as he had been in her thoughts.

Then he saw her, and he was obviously as surprised as she was.

After a silence which seemed to last a long time, in a voice that did not sound like her own Davita asked:

"Can you ... are you ... looking for ... me? Why ... are you ... here?"

The Marquis did not reply, he merely walked nearer to her until he was standing facing her.

"I should be asking that question," he said. "Why are you in the house of my Great-Aunt?"

"Your ... Great-Aunt?"

Davita repeated the words under her breath, and then she said almost frantically:

"Please ... please do not ... tell her about ... me. If you do, she will ... send me ... away. I am so happy ... here and ... safe. Please ... please!"

Even as she pleaded with him she thought it was useless and she would have to leave. Yet she knew that if he made her go, it would be like being turned out of Paradise.

"I heard you had disappeared," the Marquis said slowly, "but I certainly did not expect to find you here."

"Who . . . told you I had . . . disappeared?"

"The Prince, as it happens. I am sure your friend Violet was waiting to accept my money on your behalf."

Davita gave a little cry.

"How could you think . . . how could you . . . imagine I would . . . touch any of your . . . money?" she asked passionately. "I swear to you I had no idea what they had . . . planned or what they . . . intended to do. It was horrible . . . degrading! That is why I ran away . . . hoping they would never . . . find me, and therefore they would not be able to . . . to . . . blackmail you."

She said the dreaded word, and added:

"Perhaps . . . because I was a . . . party to their . . . plot, you will . . . want to send me to . . . prison."

Now she was trembling. Her eyes as she looked up at the Marquis were piteous.

"I think you must be well aware," he said coldly, "that I have no wish for the Police to be involved in this very reprehensible affair. The Prince discovered you had vanished, and I have not communicated with either Violet Lock or Lord Mundesley since the night of the party."

"I am glad . . . so very glad you did not . . . give them any . . . money," Davita whispered. "How did the Prince . . . discover I had . . . gone?"

"He went to your lodgings to apologise to you, as he had apologised to me, that we should have both been embroiled in anything so unpleasant in his house."

The Marquis's voice was hard as he went on:

"Mundesley tricked the Prince by pretending it was just a joke that would have no serious repercussions."

"Lord Mundesley has not . . . still got the . . . photographs?"

"The Prince took them from him and tore them up," the Marquis replied.

Davita felt a wave of relief sweep over her that was so

intense that she put down the book she was still holding
in her hand and steadied herself against a chair.

Then as the Marquis did not speak, she said in a very
small, frightened little voice:

"What are . . . you going to . . . do about . . . me?"

"What do you expect me to do?" he enquired.

"I suppose you . . . will want me to . . . leave," Davita
said dully. "Please . . . if so, do not tell your . . . Great-
Aunt what . . . happened."

"Why should she not know the truth?"

"Because it would upset and shock her, as it . . . shocked
me."

"Do you really mind what she thinks?"

"Of course I do!" Davita replied. "She has been
so . . . kind to me . . . so very . . . very kind. Only just now
she said I was . . . like the . . . daughter she had . . .
never . . . had."

As Davita spoke, the tears that had been in her eyes
overflowed and ran down her cheeks. She made no effort
to wipe them away and merely said in a broken voice:

"If you will say . . . nothing, I will make some . . . excuse
to explain my . . . having to . . . leave."

"What excuse will you give?" the Marquis enquired.

Davita made a helpless little gesture with her hands.

"I could say I must go . . . back to . . . Scotland. But as
the Countess knows my home is . . . gone, I would have
to . . . think of something very . . . convincing, but I am
not . . . certain what it . . . can be."

Now the tears ran from her cheeks down the front of
her gown.

Davita groped for her handkerchief which was concealed
in her waistband, and she wiped them away, thinking
despairingly as she did so that once again she was alone
and frightened.

Unexpectedly the Marquis said:

"Suppose we sit down and you tell me a little more
about your circumstances."

Because it was more of a command than a request, Davita obediently followed him to the ornate marble mantelpiece.

There was a sofa and several arm-chairs grouped round the hearth. She sat down on the edge of the sofa, feeling as if her fairy-tale world had collapsed round her in ruins.

"You tell me you have been happy here," the Marquis remarked.

"Very . . . very . . . happy."

"I have already learnt your father was Sir Iain Kilcraig and Violet was the daughter of your Stepmother. Why did you come to London? Did you intend to go on the stage?"

"No, I never wanted to do that," Davita answered. "Mama would have been . . . shocked at the . . . idea."

"Then why did you not stay in Scotland?"

"I had to find employment of some sort, because there was no money after Papa's debts were paid. I thought it would be easier to find something to do in London than in Edinburgh."

"So you came to ask Violet to help you?"

"There was no-one else," Davita replied. "Mama's re-lations all lived in the Western Isles and I never met them."

"I learnt your mother was a MacLeod," the Marquis said, as if he had spoken to himself.

Davita wondered why he had been interested, and then she thought in a kind of horror that he had made enquiries about her because he believed she was black-mailing him.

"I never . . . meant," she said in a frightened little voice, "to have . . . anything to do with the . . . Gaiety or . . . someone like . . . like . . . Lord Mundesley."

The way she spoke made the Marquis look at her sharply.

"Why do you speak of Mundesley like that?" he enquired.

"Because he is horrible . . . disgusting, and . . . wicked!"
Davita answered passionately.

"What did he do to you to make you feel like that
about him?"

Davita did not reply, but the Marquis saw the colour
rise in her cheeks.

"I asked you a question, Davita, I want an answer!"

She wanted to say she could not speak of it, but somehow because he was looking at her and waiting, she felt
that he compelled her to reply to his question.

"He . . . offered me a . . . house in . . . Chelsea," she said
in a voice that was almost inaudible.

"It does not surprise me," the Marquis said. "Mundesley
is a bounder and no decent woman would associate with
him."

It was what Davita felt herself. Because she was ashamed
of what she had had to tell the Marquis, she could only
sit with her hands clasped together and her head bowed.

"Forget him," the Marquis said sharply.

"I want to, because he . . . frightens . . . me."

It struck her that if she had to leave Sherburn House,
Lord Mundesley might find her again!

She thought the only thing she could do would be to
go back to Scotland and stay with Hector until Mr. Stirling
found her some sort of employment.

Because the idea seemed bleak and depressing, she
lifted her head to look at the Marquis as she said pleadingly:

"How . . . soon do you . . . want me to . . . leave?"

"I have not said that you should do so."

There was just a flicker of hope in her eyes, and then
she said, as if it was the other alternative:

"You do not . . . intend to tell your Great-Aunt . . . about
me and . . . make her . . . dismiss me?"

"I promise you I will say nothing to upset my Great-
Aunt."

"But you still . . . mean me to . . . go away?"

"Not if you wish to stay."

Davita's whole face lit up.

"Do you mean . . . are you saying," she stammered incoherently, "that I can stay here?"

For a moment the Marquis did not answer.

Davita added pleadingly:

"Please . . . please let me. I can only say how very . . . very sorry I am for what . . . happened at the . . . party."

"I believe now that you had nothing to do with it," the Marquis said kindly.

"As I told you, I had no idea . . . what they had . . . planned," Davita answered. "At the same time, I suppose if I had accepted what Lord Mundesley . . . suggested, it would not have . . . happened. Also, Violet was angry because she . . . guessed what he . . . felt about . . . me."

She stammered a little over her explanation. She felt somehow she had to be completely honest with the Marquis.

"Forget it," he said. "One day someone—and I hope it will be myself—will give Mundesley the lesson he deserves. Until that happens, put him out of your mind."

"That is what I want to do," Davita replied simply.

"Then do it!" the Marquis commanded.

"And I can stay . . . here with the . . . Countess?"

"As far as I am concerned. I imagine it is an acceptable arrangement, both for you and my Great-Aunt. She has certainly had a great number of failures with her Companions until now."

"She said they were like . . . frightened rabbits," Davita said with just a faint smile.

"You are not frightened?" the Marquis asked.

"Not of the Countess, only of you. I thought you would be very . . . very . . . angry with . . . me."

"I was very angry," the Marquis answered. "But not particularly with you, especially after I knew you had disappeared."

"You did realise that I had no intention of taking any money from you?"

"I thought that might be the reason you had gone away."

Davita gave a deep sigh.

"I am so glad you thought that. In a way, it makes everything much better, even though I never want to think about it or anything to do with the Gaiety again."

"The Gaiety?" the Marquis said in a puzzled voice.

"It is all part of a . . . world and . . . people that I do not . . . understand," Davita explained. "Katie, my Step-mother, was kind to me, and so was Violet, but at the same time they . . . shocked me."

As she spoke, she thought of Katie going away with Harry, and of Violet accepting the sables and gowns from Lord Mundesley.

"How old are you?" the Marquis asked.

"Eighteen," Davita replied.

"And you had never been away from Scotland until you came South?"

Davita shook her head.

"I had just arrived the night you saw me at Romano's, and everything was very . . . strange."

As she spoke, she remembered that what had been particularly strange had been the way Rosie had behaved. Once again she could not meet the Marquis's eyes, and the colour rose in her cheeks.

"Forget it," he said again sharply, as if he knew what she was thinking. "You should never have got mixed up in the world you call 'the Gaiety.' I can understand now why you want to stay here."

"I may really . . . stay?" Davita asked, as if she were half-afraid that he would change his mind.

"Certainly, as far as I am concerned!"

"Oh, thank you, thank you. You may think perhaps it is an . . . impertinence, but the Countess is like a . . .

Grandmother to me and I love being with . . . her. Every day here has been happier than the last."

As she spoke, she saw that the Marquis was looking at her penetratingly.

It was as if he found it hard to believe that, being so young, she was as happy as she said she was, living in the house alone with an old woman and no young people of her own age.

Davita's eyes, however, shone with an unmistakable sincerity.

After a moment he said:

"I came here to ask my Great-Aunt if I may stay the night. I only heard yesterday that there are some horses for sale in the neighbourhood, and I wish to see them. I thought too it was an opportunity to pay my respects to someone I have neglected somewhat remissibly for the last three months."

"I am sure the Countess will be very thrilled to see you," Davita replied, "but she is resting for another hour."

"That is what the servants told me," the Marquis answered. "I was going to read the papers which I understood were here in the Library, and then visit the stables."

"I was going to do that too," Davita said. "I love the horses and I feed them every afternoon."

"Then suppose we go there together," the Marquis suggested. "I have a feeling my cousin's horses are under-exercised and under-fed in his absence. If they are, I shall certainly reprimand his Head Groom."

Davita gave a little cry.

"Oh, you mustn't do that! Yates is such a conscientious man, and I promise you the horses are exercised every morning."

"By you?" the Marquis enquired.

"I have been allowed to help him since I have been here. It was been wonderful for me. I have never ridden such magnificent animals before."

"I see you have made yourself very much at home."

The Marquis's voice was mocking.

"Perhaps you think I am . . . imposing on the Countess . . . but I . . . swear to you she . . . suggested in the first place I should . . . ride and do all the . . . other things I have been . . . allowed to do."

The Marquis did not reply, and Davita wondered apprehensively if he thought she was pushing herself forward, asking favours to which she was not entitled.

'It is not surprising he disapproves of me,' she thought miserably.

Then the Marquis smiled as he said:

"Come along. What are we waiting for?"

She felt as if the sun had come out.

* * *

Later that evening Davita felt as if once again she had stepped into a dream, and that this time there was no chance of it ending in a nightmare.

It had been the Countess who suggested that she should join the Marquis for dinner.

"I am sure my great-nephew would not wish to dine alone," she had said. "And it would be a chance for you to have someone young to talk to."

"Perhaps His Lordship will not want . . . me," Davita said nervously.

"Of course he will want you," the Countess said positively. "He has a reputation of always being surrounded by attractive women."

Davita was quite certain that the Marquis did not think she was attractive. She was not surprised, when she compared herself to the beauty of Rosie, even though he had grown tired of her.

However, there was no reason why she should not do what the Countess suggested, and she was supposed to have met the Marquis today for the first time.

She therefore went to change before dinner, feeling

uncertain as to whether or not she was looking forward to
the evening.

"Suppose he is bored and is contemptuous of me?" she
asked herself.

It was, however, a consolation to feel that she could
wear a new evening-gown that she had made herself
from a sketch in *The Ladies Journal*.

It was Banks who had found some very pretty material
that had been put away years ago in the cupboard and
never made up.

It was Banks, too, who had found a sketch of the gown
that was described as having come from Paris, and it
seemed to Davita as pretty as, if not prettier than, anything that had been worn by the Gaiety Girls.

She had cut it out and made it in the Sewing-Room
after the Countess had gone to bed.

Now she was wearing it for the first time and she was
glad it looked so very different from the evening-gown in
which the Marquis had first seen her.

She could never think of her mother's wedding-dress
of Brussels lace without a little shudder.

But her new gown was spring-green gauze, the colour
of her eyes, with chiffon drapes round the low back of the
bodice, and a sash of green velvet encircled her tiny
waist.

Although she was unaware of it, Davita looked the
very embodiment of Spring.

Banks brushed her hair for her until the red lights
shone like little flames of fire, and when she was ready
she went into the Countess's bedroom to say "good-
night."

"Is that the dress you made yourself?" the Dowager
asked.

"Banks found the material that you bought in Paris
over ten years ago," Davita answered. "Do tell me if you
like it."

"It looks very attractive," the Countess replied, "and so do you, my dear. Fetch my jewel-case."

The Countess's jewel-case, large and heavy, was made of polished leather and stood on the dressing-table.

Davita carried it to the bed and the Countess opened it.

Davita thought the flashing jewels that filled it made it look like something out of Aladdin's Cave.

The Countess searched first the top tray and then the second, until at the very bottom she found what she wanted.

"I wore this when I was your age," she said. "Put it on. I want to see it round your neck."

It was a delicate necklace with small emeralds and diamonds fashioned in the shape of flowers.

Excitedly Davita ran to the mirror on the dressing-table and clasped it round her neck. It gave a finish, she thought, to her whole appearance, and also accentuated the whiteness of her skin.

"It is lovely!" she exclaimed. "May I really wear it tonight? I will be very careful with it."

"It is a present."

"A present?" Davita gasped. "I cannot take it, it is too valuable! You must not give me any more than you have given me already."

"I want you to have it," the Countess said. "I shall be very hurt if you refuse to accept it."

"Thank you, thank you," Davita answered. "You are so kind to me. I haven't any words to tell you how grateful I am."

She lifted the Countess's hand as she spoke and kissed it, and then she said:

"One day perhaps I shall be able to repay what you have done for me. I do not know quite how I shall do so."

There were tears in her eyes as she spoke, and the Countess replied:

"Run along, child, and enjoy yourself, you are making me feel sentimental."

Smiling, Davita ran downstairs where she knew the Marquis would be waiting for her in the Blue Drawing-Room. He was looking magnificent as he had the first night she had seen him in his evening-clothes.

Because he had watched her with the usual rather cynical expression on his face as she walked towards him, he made her feel very shy.

Then because what had happened was too exciting to keep to herself, she said:

"Please look at what your Great-Aunt has just given me. I feel I ought not to accept, but she said she would be very . . . hurt if I did not do so."

Then as she spoke, Davita thought she had made a mistake. Maybe the Marquis thought she was like Violet, getting presents out of men or anyone whose generosity she could impose on.

To her relief, the Marquis merely replied:

"It is certainly very suitable with your green eyes."

"You do not think it . . . wrong of me to accept such a . . . valuable present?"

"I think after what my Great-Aunt said about you to me this afternoon, it would be unkind of you not to do so."

Davita's face seemed to light up as if there were suddenly a thousand lights blazing in the room.

"Now I feel happy about . . . accepting it," she replied. "She is so . . . so kind to me, and I do want to make her . . . happy."

During dinner, although Davita had been apprehensive that she might bore him, there were so many things to talk about that time seemed to speed past on wings.

They first talked of Scotland and the Marquis told Davita how he went grouse-shooting every August and how many salmon he had caught the previous year.

"Ours is not a famous river," Davita said. "But once

Papa caught fifteen in a day, and another time I caught ten."

"I call that a very good catch," the Marquis said with a smile.

But she knew he was delighted as a sportsman that his best day had been nineteen.

"I wonder what horses you will buy tomorrow?" she asked as dinner came to an end.

"I will be able to tell you that tomorrow evening," he answered.

"You will come back after the sale?"

"I have no wish to make the journey back to London late in the evening if I am not able to bid early in the day for the horses I want."

"I will be very eager to hear all about your purchases."

"I might even bring them back with me," the Marquis said. "Two of my grooms are meeting me at the sale."

"That would be even more exciting!" Davita exclaimed.

The Marquis smiled a little mockingly.

"I am not certain that is really a compliment."

For the moment she did not understand what he meant. Then she realised that she had implied that his horses were more interesting than he was.

A little shyly, because she was uncertain how he would take the question, she asked:

"Do you . . . like being . . . flattered?"

"Only if it is sincere," the Marquis answered. "Then of course I appreciate it."

"I should have thought it would not matter to you what anyone thought about you."

"Why should you think that?"

"I suppose it is because you seem so important . . . so authoritative and . . . "

Davita stopped, afraid that what she was about to say was rude.

The Marquis did not leave that unchallenged.

"And what?" he enquired.

"I have . . . forgotten what I was going to . . . say."

"That is not true!" he said. "And I would like you to finish the sentence."

As if once again he compelled her, Davita said shyly:

"When I saw you that first night at . . . Romano's I thought that you seemed cynical and a little . . . contemptuous of everything that was going on round you. Was I right?"

The Marquis looked at her in surprise.

"In a sense," he answered. "But I did not realise it was so obvious."

"Perhaps it would not have been to everyone, but you must not forget that the Scots are fey."

The Marquis laughed.

"So you were aware I was feeling at odds with the world—that particular world in which we met."

As she thought he was referring to Rosie, Davita merely nodded her head.

The Marquis seemed to hesitate. Then he said:

"It is not something I should discuss ordinarily with someone of your age, but because you were at Romano's that night and were indirectly involved in a scene that should never have taken place, I will tell you the background of the story."

There was a hard note in his voice, and Davita said quickly:

"There is no . . . reason for you to do so. It is not for me to . . . criticise, but you did . . . ask me what I . . . felt."

"What you felt was perhaps what no-one else would. So I intend to explain to you why I was in such an unpleasant mood."

As he paused for a moment, Davita thought it was a very strange conversation for her to be having with the Marquis. But then the whole evening, she realised, was strange.

They were alone, for one thing, sitting at a candle-lit table in the huge Dining-Room, hung with paintings of the Sherburn ancestors. They were isolated on a little island of light as if they had embarked together on an unknown sea into an unknown future.

It flashed through her mind that that was indeed just what they were doing!

Then she told herself she was being ridiculously imaginative and she must listen attentively to what the Marquis was saying.

"Because you have been impelled into a world of which most girls of your age and breeding have no knowledge whatsoever," he began, "you were doubtless unaware, even before Lord Mundesley made his objectionable proposal to you, that men as a rule do not marry actresses but enjoy them as companions in a very different manner."

Davita understood that he meant gentlemen took them as mistresses.

She could not help thinking it would have been far better if that was what her father had done rather than marry Katie, who had run away to be the mistress of Harry.

"I thought Rosie very beautiful," the Marquis was saying, "which indeed she is. It was only after she accepted my protection, as it is usually called, that I discovered that she was incapable of being faithful to her protector, even though it is an unwritten law that that is what is expected of a woman in such circumstances."

He spoke in such an impersonal manner that Davita did not feel embarrassed. She was only interested as he went on:

"I found it impossible to continue providing a house for a woman who entertained in my absence a series of ne'er-do-wells who drank my wine and smoked my cigars, and as they did so felt that they were having the laugh of me."

He paused before he continued:

"That is the whole story in a nutshell. Rosie broke the rules of the game, and I brought the game to an end."

"You do not really . . . think she would have . . . killed herself?" Davita asked almost in a whisper.

The Marquis shook his head.

"It is a trick women of her class use very frequently both here and in Paris, to get their own way."

He saw the question in Davita's eyes and added:

"If you feel at all worried about Rosie's future, I learnt before I left London that she was already very comfortably settled in another house—this time in Regent's Park—which belongs to a member of the House of Lords who is frequently away from London for long intervals."

The Marquis did not give Davita a chance to say anything and merely said quietly:

"Now that I have explained that, the whole subject is a closed chapter. We will neither of us refer to it again."

Davita gave a little sigh.

"I am glad you told me."

"I only wish I did not have to do so," the Marquis said. "Do you remember my advice that night?"

"That I should go back to Scotland?" Davita asked. "What you were really saying is that I should not have come South in the first place."

She glanced at the Marquis a little uncertainly as she said:

"Even after all the . . . awful things that . . . happened . . . I am glad I did. If I had not, I should never have come to Sherburn House and would not be . . . sitting here with . . . you at this . . . moment."

"You are glad you are?" the Marquis enquired.

"But of course I am very glad. It is very exciting for me," Davita answered.

Then as her eyes met his, perhaps it was a trick of the candlelight, but she found it hard to look away.

* * *

The next day the Marquis left early to go to the sale. He sent a message to his Great-Aunt to say he was looking forward to seeing her that evening, and he hoped she had passed a restful night as he had.

Davita was with the Countess when the message was brought to her, and she laughed.

"I am sure it is a most unusual occurrence for my great-nephew to spend a restful night," she said. "From all I hear, if he is not escorting some beautiful actress from the Gaiety Theatre, he is dancing attendance on one of the beauties who surround the Prince of Wales at Marlborough House."

She spoke with a note of satisfaction in her voice, which made Davita feel she was proud that the Marquis could prove himself to be what Violet and Katie had called a "dasher."

This she had learnt was the highest grade a young man about town could reach.

"Then he must have been very bored with me last night," Davita told herself with a sigh.

Nevertheless, the Marquis had not appeared bored. They had sat talking for a long time over dinner and then had gone on talking when they retired to the Blue Drawing-Room.

To her surprise, he had been as easy to talk to on any number of subjects as her father had been before he had married Katie and started drinking.

Davita had gone to bed thinking over what they had said, and had planned what she would say as a challenge when she had the chance to talk with him another evening.

"Even if he was bored," she told herself, "he is coming back tonight, and even if I never see him again, I shall have quite a lot to remember."

It was a warm day, and she went riding for an hour in the morning, while the Countess was having massage on her legs from an experienced masseur who came from Oxford to treat her.

Wearing her smart new habit, Davita could not help wishing that the Marquis could see her and they could ride together.

Then she told herself that wishing things was just a waste of time, and he would doubtless think her a very poor horsewoman beside those he rode with in Rotten Row or in his estate in Hertfordshire.

The Countess had told her how fine it was.

"You would certainly approve of my great-nephew's house. It was restored in the middle of the Eighteenth Century and a great part of it is much older than that."

"I know I would not love it as much as I love this house," Davita had replied loyally.

"Nevertheless, get him to tell you about it," the Countess said. "He is very proud of his ancestry. I have told him for years that it is time he was married and had a family."

Davita was surprised at the strange feeling the Countess's words gave her. It was almost like a physical pain.

Then she thought wistfully how fortunate the Marquis's wife would be, not because she would have a fine house and a grand estate but because she would be able to talk to him and learn from him so much that was interesting.

'If only he would stay here a week,' she thought wistfully. 'I would be very much wiser and better informed by the time he left.'

She assumed that tomorrow, perhaps early in the morning, he would go back to London and, though she tried not to put it into words, the house would seem empty without him.

There was still tonight, and she wished she had another dress to wear.

'Not that he would notice me if I were dressed up like the Queen of Sheba,' she thought mockingly.

The hours of the day seemed to pass slowly, and when the Countess went to rest, Davita went out into the sunshine.

Instead of going down to the lake as she always did, she went to the stables.

"Have you room for the horses His Lordship may bring back with him from the sale?" she asked Yates, the Head Groom.

"There's places for a dozen more 'orses, Miss," he replied. "But I don't think 'is Lordship'll bring more than two or three."

"I am sure they will be very fine animals," Davita remarked.

"They will," Yates agreed. " 'Is Lordship be a first-class judge of 'orseflesh."

Davita fed the horses as she always did with carrots and apples, and made a fuss of each one.

Then she walked from the stables into the courtyard outside the front door, and down the first part of the drive towards the bridge which spanned the lake.

She stood for a long time, leaning on the greystone to look into the water below and watch the fish flashing over the gravel bottom.

She walked under the shadow of the great oak trees, a little way up the drive, and although she would not admit it to herself, she half-hoped she might meet the Marquis returning from the sale.

She was almost halfway to the lodges when she saw a carriage turn in at them. Her leart leapt; the Marquis was returning, and far sooner than she had expected.

She stood still, watching the horses approach, but as they drew near she was aware that it was not the open curricle that was coming towards her which the Marquis had been driving when he had left that morning.

Instead it was a closed brougham, and she thought with a feeling of disappointment that it must be someone coming to call on the Countess.

Quickly, because the horses were drawing near, she turned and walked away from the drive into the Park.

She heard the horses pass, and deliberately did not

look round but went on walking to where she could see a cluster of spotted deer in the shade of one of the larger trees.

She was wondering how near she could get to them without their being afraid, when her instinct, or perhaps her sixth sense, made her aware that someone was behind her.

She had heard no sound because of the thick grass. She turned round apprehensively, then was frozen to the spot on which she was standing.

Striding towards her, florid and flamboyant, was Lord Mundesley!

Chapter Seven

Davita was frozen into immobility as she stared at Lord Mundesley, thinking he could not be real.

But there was no mistaking his swaggering walk, his top-hat set at a jaunty angle, and the carnation in his button-hole.

Only when he reached her side did she think of running away, but then it was too late.

"So here you are!" he said in a tone of satisfaction. "It has taken me a long time to find you; but now I am successful, as I always am."

"What do you want . . . what are you . . . doing?" Davita managed to say, feeling almost as if she had choked on the words.

"I want you," Lord Mundesley replied, "as I always have. If you thought I had forgotten what you look like, you are very much mistaken."

"Leave me . . . alone!" Davita cried. "You have no . . . right here. I have no wish to see . . . you or Violet ever . . . again."

Lord Mundesley smiled unpleasantly, and his eyes, looking at her in a way that always made her feel shy, were now somehow menacing.

Then as if her face, which was very pale, her red hair, and her green eyes moved him irresistibly, there was a note of passion in his voice as he said:

"I want you, Davita! I have wanted you since I first saw you, and I mean to have you!"

She gave a little startled cry, and he went on:

"You do not suppose the Countess of Sherburn, who is a very respectable old lady, would keep you as her Companion if I tell her of your behaviour in London or that you are very closely connected with the Gaiety."

"You are ... blackmailing ... me!"

She meant to speak angrily and accusingly because Lord Mundesley frightened her as he always had, but her voice sounded weak, and he could see that she was trembling.

"I have spent a lot of money on detectives who have finally tracked you down," he said. "Now that I have found you, I suggest you behave like a sensible girl and come back with me to London. I will look after you as I always intended to do."

Now Davita gave a small scream, like an animal that had been trapped, and turned to run away. It was too late!

Lord Mundesley reached out, caught hold of her wrists when she was in the very act of moving, and as she struggled to be free, he pulled her relentlessly into his arms.

"Let me go ... let me go!" she cried.

She knew even as she fought against him that her resistance excited him, and he was also very strong.

"I will teach you to obey me," he said, "and to love me."

"I hate you ... I hate you!" she tried to say.

But the words were strangled in her throat, because she was aware that his face was very near to hers and he was about to kiss her.

It was then that she screamed again, fighting with every ounce of her strength, but knowing it must be ineffective.

Suddenly a furious voice shouted:

"What the devil do you think you are doing!"

Then she knew that at the very last moment—the eleventh hour—she was saved.

Lord Mundesley's arms holding her slackened, and she managed to twist herself free of him. But because she was breathless and weak from fear, she stumbled and collapsed to the ground.

As she did so, she heard the Marquis say:

"It is time you were taught a lesson, Mundesley, and this time I will see that you have it."

As he spoke he struck out at Lord Mundesley, who stepped backwards to protect himself, while his hat fell off his head.

As he put up his fists to defend himself, the Marquis struck him again. This time he staggered but did not fall.

"Damn you, Vange!" he exclaimed. "If you want to fight, do so, but in a gentlemanly fashion—with pistols."

"You are no gentleman," the Marquis retorted. "And you do not behave like one."

He advanced on Lord Mundesley again, who attempted to fend him off.

But the Marquis slipped under his guard, caught him on the point of the chin, and he crashed to the ground.

For a moment he was stunned, and then as he opened his eyes the Marquis standing over him said:

"Get out of here or I swear you will be carried out on a stretcher!"

Lord Mundesley let out a foul oath.

The Marquis continued:

"I am letting you off lightly because of your age, but if you ever approach Davita again I will thrash you within an inch of your life. Is that clear?"

Lord Mundesley swore again, but the Marquis did not wait to listen to it. He turned to Davita, who was still sitting on the ground with a stricken look in her eyes.

The Marquis pulled her to her feet, and as she swayed weakly against him, he picked her up in his arms and carried her back through the trees to the drive.

She was trembling as he did so, but at the same time his arms were the most comforting thing she had ever known.

Drawn up behind Lord Mundesley's brougham was the Marquis's chaise.

He put Davita down gently in the seat, got in beside her, and, taking the reins from the groom who had been holding the horses, said:

"Walk home, Jim."

"Very good, M'Lord."

The Marquis drove his horses away down the drive without even glancing in the direction of where he had left Lord Mundesley.

As he approached the lake he did not cross the bridge which led to the house, but instead drove along a grass track which led to the end of the lake where there was a wood.

When they were out of sight of the house, the Marquis drew the horses to a standstill, fixed the reins to the dashboard, and turned to look at Davita.

She was sitting in the corner of the chaise where he had placed her, her fingers clenched together, and there was still a stricken expression in her eyes.

At the same time, she was not trembling so violently.

"It is all right," the Marquis said quietly. "You are safe!"

It was then that Davita gave a little cry and burst into tears.

"He will . . . take his . . . revenge," she sobbed. "He will . . . tell the Countess about . . . me, and I shall . . . have to go . . . away. He will . . . never let me . . . go."

Her words were almost incoherent, but the Marquis heard them. Very gently, as if he was afraid he would frighten her, he put his arms round her and drew her close to him.

She was so distressed she hardly realised what he was doing, and went on crying against his shoulder.

"I told you it was all right," he said quietly. "Mundesley will do none of those things. I will not let him."

"How . . . can you . . . stop him? He had . . . detectives looking for me. Everywhere I . . . hide, they will . . . find me."

There was a note of despair in her voice, and as she spoke Davita had pictures of herself running . . . running with Lord Mundesley pursuing her as if she were a fox.

"Stop crying," the Marquis said. "I want to talk to you."

It struck Davita that perhaps this was the last time she would ever be able to talk to him.

With what was almost a superhuman effort, she attempted to control her tears, and groped in her waist-band for her handkerchief.

The Marquis took one from the breast-pocket of his coat and placed it in her hands.

Because it smelt of eau-de-Cologne, and because it was his, it made her want to cry again.

She wiped the tears from her cheeks and though they were still swimming in her eyes and her eye-lashes were wet, she looked at him, feeling she should move from the shelter of his arms, but making no effort to do so.

He looked down at her and said gently:

"You look as if you are very much in need of someone to look after you."

Davita shuddered, and he knew she was thinking it might be Lord Mundesley.

"How could I have anticipated that this would happen to you?" the Marquis asked. "And yet I came home early because I had an idea I was needed."

"I needed you desperately," Davita whispered, "and

somehow I . . . thought you might be . . . earlier than
was . . . expected."

"Was that why you were walking on the drive?" the
Marquis asked.

Because he might think it forward of her, she looked
down shyly, and could not answer him.

"I came in time," the Marquis said, as if he was following his own train of thought. "And now, as I have said,
Lord Mundesley will not trouble you again."

His words brought the fear back, and Davita cried:

"But he will . . . and how can you . . . prevent him when
you have . . . gone away?"

"By taking you with me," the Marquis said very quietly.

She thought she could not have heard him aright.

As her eyes looked up at him enquiringly, he said:

"It is too soon—I did not mean to tell you about it yet,
Davita, but ever since I first saw you I have been unable
to forget you, and I think perhaps you know already that
we mean something very special to each other."

For the moment Davita thought she must be dreaming,
but then as the Marquis seemed to be enveloped with a
dazzling light, she thought that perhaps he was making
her the same proposal as Lord Mundesley had.

With an inarticulate little sound she turned her face
away from him.

As if he knew without words what she was thinking, he
said:

"I am suggesting that the only way you can be completely
safe for the rest of your life is to marry me."

For a moment Davita could only hold her breath. Then
she said in a voice that did not sound like her own:

"Did you . . . ask me to . . . marry you?"

"I will keep you safe," the Marquis replied, "not only
from Mundesley but from anyone like him, and I promise, my darling, one thing I will never allow you to do is
to go behind the stage at the Gaiety or have supper at
Romano's."

He was smiling at her as he spoke, with a look in his eyes which made him appear no longer cynical or contemptuous but very different.

"It can . . . not be . . . true!"

Davita was trembling, and her eyes were shining as if the same light she had seen envelop the Marquis was radiating from her.

"I will have to make you believe it," he said, "but first I want to know what you feel about me."

"You cannot . . . marry me," she murmured. "You are so . . . magnificent, as I thought the first time I . . . saw you, and when I thought more about you I knew you were . . . everything a . . . man should . . . be."

"You thought about me?" the Marquis asked.

"How could I . . . help it? And after that . . . terrible party, I thought you would . . . hate me."

"I suspected you could have had nothing to do with such a despicable plot," the Marquis said, "and when you disappeared I was certain of it."

"I wanted to . . . ask you to . . . forgive me long before you came . . . here."

"I will forgive you," the Marquis said, "if you tell me what you feel about me now."

Davita leant forward, and hiding her face against his shoulder she whispered:

"I love . . . you. I did not . . . realise it was . . . love . . . but I kept thinking about you, and when you . . . talked to me last night I knew to be with you was the most . . . wonderful thing that had . . . ever . . . happened to me."

"You will always be with me in the future."

As the Marquis spoke he put his fingers under her chin and gently turned her face up to his. As he did so, he felt her tremble, but he knew it was not with fear.

He looked down at her face for a long moment, as if he wished to engrave it on his memory forever, then as his arms tightened his lips sought hers.

It was as if the Heavens opened, and she knew an

inexpressible ecstasy that was beyond all thought or imagination.

The touch of the Marquis's lips seemed to give her all the beauty she had sought in her dreams, all the wonder that she had known could only be found in love, and thought it would never be hers.

He kissed her gently at first, as if she was something infinitely precious, then the softness of her mouth aroused him in a way he had never known before.

His kiss became more possessive, more insistent, and yet Davita was not afraid.

She knew that she belonged to him, and she surrendered herself to his strength and the vibrations which came from him to link with the vibrations from herself.

She felt as if he took not only her body into his keeping, but her heart and her soul. They were his and she knew that her love for him, and his for her, was not only very human but also part of the Divine.

When finally the Marquis raised his head, she said a little incoherently, but with a note of indescribable rapture in her voice:

"I love you . . . I love you!"

"And I love you, my sweet darling," the Marquis replied.

"How can you love me when there are so many really . . . beautiful women in your . . . life?"

She was thinking of the Gaiety Girls as she spoke. Of Rosie and Violet, of Lottie Collins, and also the social beauties that the Countess had said pursued him.

The Marquis held her very closely against him.

"When I first saw you sitting in the Box," he said, "I knew you were different from anyone I had ever seen before."

"In the Box?" Davita asked in a puzzled voice.

"I was looking round the Theatre with my Opera-glasses," he explained. "And I saw you watching the Show, with the excitement of a child at her first Pantomime."

"I had no . . . idea you were . . . there."

The Marquis smiled.

"I found you more entrancing than any Show I have ever seen, and when later I saw you in Romano's, I found you were even lovelier than you had appeared at a distance."

"You . . . told me to go . . . back to . . . Scotland!"

"I could not bear you to be spoilt, and to think of you losing that young, untouched look, which is the most beautiful thing I have ever seen in my life."

As if he could not help himself, he bent his head and kissed her again, and as he felt Davita's instinctive response, he said a long time later, and his voice was unsteady:

"I have so much to teach you, my darling, and you have so much to learn about love. Thank God you ran away when you did."

"I . . . thought I would . . . never see you . . . again."

"I thought the same thing—you haunted me. If Mundesley was looking for you, so was I."

He gave a little laugh.

"Fate played into my hands—I found you where I least expected to—in the Library of Sherburn House."

"I thought you would . . . send me . . . away."

"I was overjoyed at finding you. At the same time, I had to make sure that you were not implicated in any way in Mundesley's disgraceful act of vengeance."

"I was so . . . ashamed."

"I told you to forget it! At the same time, my precious little love, we must be thankful that however reprehensible it was to be mixed up with such people, it brought us together."

"You are . . . quite certain that I can . . . marry you?" Davita asked. "Perhaps the Countess and your other relatives will . . . disapprove."

"I think my Great-Aunt will be delighted," the Marquis replied, "even though she will regret losing you, and the rest of my relatives do not matter, although they will be pleased I am doing what they have urged me to do for a long time."

"They . . . wanted you to be . . . married?"

"They wanted me to have a wife and an heir."

Davita blushed and hid her face against him.

"Do I make you shy?" the Marquis enquired.

"Yes . . . but I am also very . . . very proud . . . I still cannot believe that what you are saying is . . . true."

"I will make you believe it," the Marquis said.

Once again he would have kissed her, but Davita put up her hands to stop him.

"There is something I want to . . . say to you."

"What is it?" he asked.

"You have asked me to . . . marry you. It is the most glorious . . . perfect thing which can ever happen, but are you certain . . . absolutely certain that I will not . . . bore you?"

For a moment the Marquis did not answer and she went on:

"It would be an unbearable agony if I lost you now, but it would be worse . . . very much worse . . . if I lost you after I became your . . . wife. In fact, I think then I would . . . really want to . . . die."

As she spoke, she felt she was saying almost the same thing as Rosie had said, and yet it was a cry that came from her heart.

The Marquis gave her such a sense of security that she knew that when she was in his arms she would never feel afraid again. At the same time, he already filled her whole world, and she knew that once they were married he would fill the sky as well.

Without him there would only be darkness!

As if what she was thinking was reflected in her eyes, and the Marquis could read her thoughts, he said:

"It is difficult to explain to you, my sweet, but although I was not really aware of it, I have been looking for you all my life. I thought it was impossible to find a woman

who was intelligent enough to stimulate my mind and at
the same time be pure, innocent, and untouched, and
very different in every way from the women with whom I
amused myself."

He drew Davita closer as he said:

"When I saw you at first sitting in the Box, and the
next time at Romano's, it was almost as if you were
enveloped with light. I knew you were what I had always
wanted."

Davita gave a little start when he said the word "light."
As if she knew he wanted her to explain, she said:

"Just now when you said you . . . wished to . . . marry
me, there was light blazing all round you, and I knew it
was the . . . light that came from . . . God."

"My darling—my sweet," the Marquis said in his deep
voice. "We think alike. We are perhaps fey about each
other, and because of it we know that we belong."

He kissed her again before she could answer, and then
as his kiss finished he looked down at her eyes shining up
at his, a faint flush on her cheeks, and her lips soft and
trembling from his kisses.

"I adore you and I want you," he said. "The sooner we
get married, the sooner you will be sure that you are
safe, and no-one will ever hurt or frighten you again. Let
us go back and tell Aunt Louise that she has to find
another Companion."

"I am afraid she will be . . . upset," Davita said.

"She will be compensated in knowing she now has a
great-niece," the Marquis smiled.

He picked up the reins. The horses, who had been
quietly grazing the grass, began to move.

He turned the chaise round skilfully. Then as they
started the drive back alongside the lake, putting one
arm round Davita, he pulled her closer to him.

"I love you, my adorable little Scot," he said, "and I
know that just as you will never lose me, I will never lose
you. We have so many exciting things to do together."

Davita put her head against his arm.

"I am so happy," she whispered, "so wildly, unbelievably happy . . . but it is like walking into a dream . . . and I want . . . you to . . . feel the same."

"I am so happy that I feel I am dreaming," the Marquis said. "At the same time, when I kiss you I know you are real—very real, and this is only the beginning of our love, which will grow and intensify all the years we are together."

Davita gave a little cry of happiness.

"How can you say such wonderful things to me?"

"It is you who make me say them," the Marquis replied. "In fact I am rather surprised at them myself."

There was just the touch of a mocking note in his voice, but it was very different from the way he had spoken when he was cynical and contemptuous.

Looking up at him, Davita thought the lines had almost vanished on his face, and he looked much younger. Then when his eyes met hers she knew he was very much in love.

They reached the end of the lake, and as the Marquis took his arm from her so that he could drive his horses over the bridge, Davita said:

"When I arrived and saw the house, I felt I could hide here in safety . . . but now I know there is only one safe place . . . and that is with . . . you."

The Marquis took his eyes from the horses to look at her, and as he smiled he said:

"My love will keep you safe, my beautiful one, now and forever."

Then as Davita put out her hand to touch him, she knew they were both enveloped with the light of love, which comes from God and sweeps away the darkness of evil.

ABOUT THE AUTHOR

BARBARA CARTLAND, the world's most famous romantic novelist, who is also an historian, playwright, lecturer, political speaker and television personality, has now written over 200 books.

She has also had many historical works published and has written four autobiographies as well as the biographies of her mother and that of her brother Ronald Cartland, who was the first Member of Parliament to be killed in the last war. This book has a preface by Sir Winston Churchill.

Barbara Cartland has sold 100 million books over the world, more than half of these in the U.S.A. She broke the world record in 1975 by writing twenty books, and her own record in 1976 with twenty-one. In addition, her album of love songs has just been published, sung with the Royal Philharmonic Orchestra.

In private life, Barbara Cartland, who is a Dame of the Order of St. John of Jerusalem, has fought for better conditions and salaries for Midwives and Nurses. As President of the Royal College of Midwives (Hertfordshire Branch), she has been invested with the first Badge of Office ever given in Great Britain which was subscribed to by the Midwives themselves. She has also championed the cause for old people and founded the first Romany Gypsy Camp in the world.

Barbara Cartland is deeply interested in Vitamin Therapy and is President of the British National Association for Health.